BY
Denise Cass Brookman

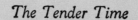

*The Tender Time*

THE TENDER TIME ঌ a story of
first love ঌ by Denise Cass Brookman
ঌ published by Macrae Smith Company

&❧ *For my parents, my husband, and my children who have given me all my tender times as adolescent and adult*

# The Tender Time

## ✎§ *Chapter one*

THIS IS HOW IT STARTED, WITH STEPHIE AND SCOTT. ON
Sunday, January twenty-eighth at two o'clock in the
afternoon, when she was a sophomore and all her sophomore friends had girl names. In a scarlet dress and ski
suit frame of mind she ran and slid across a small patch
of ice in front of the house where she was to meet him.

She was glad that if she had to ring anybody's bell, it
was to be Nancy's, because of all the people that were
going to be there she knew only Nancy. And even her
she knew only as well as any sophomore would know
any junior. Only well enough to blush and half stammer,
"I . . . I don't know. I'll ask my mother."

This, in answer to Nancy's question of a week ago,
"My father's office is having a dance, and the young
people are invited and one of his clients has a son who's
in your class, and can you go?"

Stephie found her mother in the kitchen when she
got home from school that day. Her mother looked kind
of funny when she told her, and Stephie relaxed. Everything was going to be all right. Her mother would say
no, and she wouldn't have to go. Now that she didn't
have to worry about it, she felt less conscious of herself

as a girl with legs more up and down than in and out, and freckles here and there and everywhere and green eyes she wished were blue or brown, and short just-brown hair that hung down the sides of her face like dachshund ears.

Stephie took an apple out of the bowl and bit into it. She wished it were spring at Grandfather's farm and she could settle onto the broad back of old Molly and clomp along and forget about the things that bothered her. She was wondering if Barbara's cold was better and if maybe Barbara would be allowed out of the house when her mother said, "Of course, you can go . . . Don't chomp so, Stephie. You sound like a horse."

Stephie had decided to change into jeans. She got as far as the kitchen door before she whirled around.

"What did you say?"

Her mother's back was to her as she worked at the sink.

"I said . . . of course you can go."

"You did?"

"You sound surprised."

Stephie just stood there. "Why?"

"Why what?"

She moved at last and walked over to the sink, desperation in her voice. "Why can I go? Why?"

Her mother didn't even turn around.

"I can't keep you a little girl forever."

Stephie reached over and turned off the faucet.

"But I don't want to go!"

Her mother wiped her hands on a towel.

"Why not?"

"Because . . . Because it's silly! It's mushy! I don't like

boys. All they're good for is teasing you and throwing snowballs at you and pushing you around."

"Does Barbara think it's . . . mushy, too?"

Stephie slumped in a chair and shrugged her shoulders.

"Oh, Barbara," she surprised herself by saying. "Sometimes she makes me sick. She pretends she's mad when they push her around. She screams when they pin her arms behind her back, but she really likes it."

Her mother sat down across the table from her.

"You liked Billy Rawlings. You went out with him."

"Only once. And that was different. I paid my own way in."

"Look, darling. Stephie, look at me. . . ."

Stephie reluctantly raised her eyes. She was glad she didn't have one of those sweet, floppy housedress mothers. Everyone said look at your mother and see yourself at her age. She certainly hoped when she got that old she'd look as pretty, which was pretty good for . . . gee . . . thirty-seven.

"There has to be a first time," her mother said gently. "Sometimes it isn't easy but. . . ."

Stephie was close to tears.

"But why does my first dance have to be my first date, and a blind one at that?"

"Blind?"

"Well, not exactly. I know who he is and he knows who I am, he's in one of my classes, but that's all."

"Not really all. We've known the Parkers for a long time. Not well, maybe. But we see them every so often. Why, I played bridge with Helen Parker only last week."

"I don't see why I have to go because you play bridge with his mother."

"You should go for one reason only," she began, and stopped and began again. "Mrs. Parker called today. You'll see. You'll have a wonderful time."

Stephie stared dumbly at her, knowing there was little she could do about a mother's insistence, let alone two mothers plotting together.

"I'll get you a lovely dress. Just think, your first formal."

"I won't be able to stand it," Stephie pleaded as her mother resumed her position at the sink. "The old dance is weeks away. I won't be able to do anything or have any fun in the meantime, just thinking about it." Her voice rose. "I can't go, Mother!"

Her mother was silent for a moment. "You'll get used to the idea," she said quietly.

The kitchen door whooshed open letting more wind in than Barbara who was struggling, half in, half out, to close it. She succeeded at last, flattened against it, and then turned around, gasping a little.

"Hi! What a wind! 'Lo, Mrs. Rodgers."

Stephie brightened. A friend in need, she thought. And a Best Friend is even better than just a friend. As Best Friends went, she couldn't have picked a better one than Barbara. Barbara, red hair spun fine, always looked, it seemed to Stephie, like a dancing recital fairy. She never clumped. She tiptoed in and out and around things and somehow everything always came out all right. Maybe Barbara could help her.

Her mother's voice cut into her musings.

"Barbara said hello, Stephie."

Stephie looked up and held Barbara's eyes for a moment and then switched over to her mother's.

[4]

"I bet Barbara's mother wouldn't. . . ."

Edith Rodgers sighed. "Whatever Barbara and her mother do is no concern of mine or yours."

Barbara sneezed over-vigorously. "Hurry up, Stephie," she commanded, "and get your things on! It'll be dark soon."

Mrs. Rodgers turned to Barbara and raised a questioning eyebrow.

"Are you sure your mother wants you outside with that cold?"

Barbara sniffled a little and smiled ingratiatingly.

"It's much better. Really. I'm going back to school tomorrow."

"I'm not sure either of you should be out in this wind. It's supposed to drop to fourteen tonight and it's bound to snow."

"Just over to my house," Barbara wheedled. "I've got a new record."

"Well, if you're not going to stay outdoors. . . ."

"We won't," Barbara promised, swooping on Stephie and pushing her out of the kitchen. "Hurry and get your coat!"

The Barbara magic, Stephie thought as she belted the jeans and reached for the wool jacket. Why was it that Barbara always got away with things? It made her kind of mad in a way. Sometimes she really couldn't stand her if it weren't for the fact that she was her Best Friend.

"And remember," her mother said as Stephie re-entered the kitchen, "I want you home by five thirty. Your father's going to be late tonight so we'll have an early dinner together."

Stephie merely nodded.

"Did you hear me, Stephie?"

She picked the safest of the words crowded close to the surface. "Yes," she mumbled, pulling the door open, the wind pushing the others back down deep inside her.

Barbara nodded back at the house.

"Well, I got you out of that. What's it all about? Mother's Little Girl been naughty today?"

"Nothing." Stephie carefully stepped over the cracks in the sidewalk. "And I'm not mother's little girl!"

"Trouble with you is that you don't know how to play her. You have to know when and when not to. . . ."

Stephie kicked angrily at a crack.

"All right, so I'm dumb!"

"Well, don't get mad!"

"I'm not mad!"

Barbara drew away from her.

"Well, you don't have to take it out on me."

Stephie looked stricken. She didn't know what got into her lately, what made her do it, snapping at Barbara. It would serve her right if Barbara decided not to be Best Friends any more. Then she wouldn't ever get to spend the summer at Barbara's cottage on the lake again, or laugh and whisper together, or pass each other notes in school.

Aside from that, she guessed she liked Barbara best because Barbara made everything exciting. Even ordinary things. She made every day seem like a holiday number on a calendar, red and fancy with a picture around it.

Stephie hated the times when Barbara got mad at her, though they didn't happen often because she was careful not to make them happen. But, in a way, it wasn't so

[6]

awful at all, because when Barbara got glad again, Stephie was even happier than she had been before Barbara got mad.

Stephie touched her timidly on the arm.

"I . . . I didn't mean to take it out on you."

Barbara just jerked her arm away.

The silence made almost as much noise as the wind, Stephie decided miserably as they neared Barbara's house.

"What'll we do?" Barbara asked suddenly.

Stephie stopped short, hating to ask now that Barbara was speaking again, but feeling she had to.

"I thought we were going to your house."

Barbara had already begun cutting diagonally away from her house.

"You're right. You are dumb."

"But you said. . . ."

"I know, I know. I'm saying something else now. Come on."

"But my mother . . ." Stephie began, moving after her.

". . . Just doesn't want you outside. So we won't be outside."

"We won't?"

Houses had become Bill's Barber Shop and Watch Repairs and Gas For Less.

"No," Barbara told her, stopping directly in front of Bronson's Drugstore. "We can go to The Platter Shop and listen to some records."

They had passed The Platter Shop a block back. Stephie quickly agreed, not looking at Bronson's.

Barbara began jigging. "Oh, let's go in here instead and get a Coke, I'm cold."

"We can get warm in The Platter Shop," Stephie dared to suggest.

Barbara already had her hand on the door.

"Please, Barbara. . . ."

Barbara had to turn around because Stephie hadn't moved.

"Why?"

"Because . . . because they'll probably be in there .. hanging around and . . . and you know. . . ."

Barbara put her hand on the door again.

"Well, they won't be hanging around you. They never pay any attention to you."

Stephie was too concerned over the inside of Bronson's to be overly bothered by the inside of Stephie, the hurt put there by the Barbara words. That's what she always thought of them as being, Barbara words. They were ordinary old words everybody used, but Barbara never just used words, she made them do things. They made you feel good as well as bad, and when they made you feel bad it was usually, Stephie had to admit, because it was the truth. Boys didn't pay any attention to her.

"But they might . . . now," Stephie pled to Barbara's back as she reluctantly followed her inside.

The now did it.

"Now? Why now?" Barbara asked, whirling around.

"Because they might have heard and they'll start calling out all those things that boys call out," Stephie said, rushing the words out. "Please let's go sit somewhere."

For once Barbara didn't idle at the magazine stand near the boys dangling from stools at the soda fountain. She didn't even take the long way around the boys draped over the juke box to the booth Stephie had scurried into in the back.

"Heard about what, for goodness sake?" she demanded as she hurriedly slid into the seat opposite Stephie.

"About what my mother and I were arguing about. I've got a . . ." Stephie paused and glanced quickly around the high sides of the booth, ". . . a date," she whispered. "With Scott Parker. A dance. She's making me go."

With each announcement . . . date, Scott, dance, go . . . Barbara's eyes blew open and banged not quite shut like a door in a draft.

"No," was all Barbara said, but little dots of color splotched her cheek bones.

"Yes," Stephie insisted, the awful finality of it making her voice tremble.

"I wouldn't go out with any old boy if I didn't want to!" Barbara cut her off, digging in her jeans for change. "You wouldn't catch me going out with that skinny, conceited Scott Parker." Barbara jumped up. "Cherry or plain?"

"Plain."

Stephie sat there dejectedly. Here she was getting Barbara mad all over again. This was one of those days when she couldn't do anything right. Funny, though. She was sure that one time Barbara had said she thought Scott was cute, though she was also sure that if she reminded her now she'd deny it. At least, the little she'd noticed him, he wasn't like the other boys hanging around on the steps after school and making cracks when you passed.

Barbara thumped the two Cokes on the table and

Stephie's smile fluttered and fell. They sipped in silence.

Barbara pushed hers away. "I have to go."

"Wait," Stephie begged. "What am I going to do?"

"I thought you said it was all settled."

"It is. I mean what am I going to do that night . . what should I say . . . how am I supposed to . . . to act?"

"Why ask me? I've never had a date before."

Stephie felt the panic pushing up through her.

"Yes, but you always know what to do. You'd know what to do if . . . if. . . ."

Barbara didn't help her out. "If what?"

"If he . . . tries to, to . . . you know. . . ."

Barbara said it. "Kiss you?" And Stephie was sorry she did because it was hard and sort of un-nice said right out that way. "Well you've been kissed before," Barbara added coldly.

Stephie reddened. "Oh, yes," and wondered why she lied unless it was because Barbara assumed she had at all those silly birthday parties they used to go to in grammar school.

Stephie remembered one in particular. The presents had been opened and the prizes awarded for racing with beans on a knife and dropping clothespins in a bottle and it still wasn't quite time for the refreshments. They all sat or stood stiffly, uneasily conscious of the powder and cologne and white shirts and clean fingernails, wondering what to do next. Several of the boys shuffled their feet and then one kicked a gangling boy in the seat of the pants, crying, "Pin the tail on the donkey!"

And the gangling boy, voice cracking, bounded around the recreation room yelling, hee-haw, hee-haw, hee-haw! Stephie wasn't quite sure how it happened, but suddenly

the hee-haws had turned into kissing noises and somebody above the snickering and tittering suggested playing Post Office.

She shivered a little now, recalling her turn in the
closet. She could feel again the handkerchief balled in
one moist hand, dreading that her name would be called,
dreading that it wouldn't, feeling the color squirt over
her cheeks and hearing the guffaws as she was pushed
into the stuffy cubicle.

She stood there, smashed against a bag of golf clubs,
and wasn't certain whether it was his breathing she heard
or her own. She wanted to change her position but she
was afraid to move and then she knew she'd have to
because she couldn't stand the agonizing immobility one
second longer when the voice came down loud and in-
sistent from the head of the stairs.

"Ice cream, everybody! Cake! Come on up!"

And he had bolted from the closet and left her standing there among the raincoats and golf clubs.

It was the first and last time she'd ever been left in a
closet. Thereafter, she hid in the bathroom or pretended
she had to look for her purse. Finally, she just didn't go
to the parties any more.

Stephie shook her head.

"That's different," she told Barbara. "That kind of
thing."

Barbara patted a red curl into place.

"Well, I'll tell you what I did once when. . . ."

Stephie's mouth fell open, wider than necessary to get
the words out.

"You mean you. . . ."

"Yes!" Barbara leaned over the table, tumbling out the

[11]

details. "In your gangway. Bob Carter was horsing around, not letting me through with my bike, and he held my hands and kissed me!"

"What did you do?"

"I kicked him," she announced casually, leaning back and giving the curl another pat.

"Oh . . ." Stephie gasped it. "I don't think I could . . . could do that."

Barbara shrugged. "In the movies they slap their faces."

"I know. But they really don't mean it." She pushed the Coke away from her almost violently. "I wish you were going instead of me. You'd know what to do. Besides, you're pretty and everything, and I just look healthy."

Barbara didn't disagree.

"Why didn't you tell her you wouldn't go?"

Stephie sighed. "I did. But she said I'd get used to the idea."

"I told her she'd get used to the idea," Edith Rodgers informed her husband.

Stephie, in her pajamas, half-way down the stairs to get a glass of milk, stopped and sat down, peering through the balusters at her father. She saw him lay the paper down and get up a little stiffly from the chair to put another log on the fire. He looked, she thought, like a father. That indefinable anonymous something that made all fathers look alike.

He put the poker down and turned around, rocking a little in front of the fire.

"Perhaps you're being a little hard on her, Edith," he said quietly. "After all, she's only fifteen."

"Already fifteen, you mean," her mother corrected him, snipping at the hemline of one of Stephie's skirts.

Stephie held her breath. Maybe, she thought hopefully, her father wouldn't retreat before her mother's arguments.

"What are you getting at?" Stephie heard him ask, an attentive note in his voice.

Edith Rodgers said, waving the skirt at him, "This is the second time I've had to lengthen this. And when I finish sewing and pressing it, I'll be able to wear it myself!"

Her father smiled. "She is growing, isn't she?"

"Growing, yes, but not growing up." She sank back in the chair. "Oh, Tom," her shoulders sagged, "I dislike pushing her as much as you do, but I think it's high time she begins growing emotionally."

"Why high time?"

Stephie wondered why, too, as she pressed closer against the railing.

Edith Rodgers threaded the needle on the fourth try.

"When I clean her dresser I want to find prom bids and a couple of old pressed corsages, not . . ." she jabbed the needle into the material, "not horseshoes in her underwear drawer."

Tom Rodgers' lips twitched and broadened into a grin.

"It's really not funny!"

Stephie didn't think it was, either, feeling the hot color flood her cheeks.

"Maybe it isn't," her father said, some of the smile still there, "but it isn't tragic, either, that she likes horses at the moment better than boys. It's a little early to find a dresser full of prom bids."

Mrs. Rodgers put the skirt aside with a sigh. "She's

[13]

like you . . . shy, sensitive. She's getting to the age when she won't come to me or you with her problems. Right now she wants to be independent and dependent at the same time. It's the same way with boys. She loathes and likes them simultaneously."

Tom Rodgers was more than a good listener. He looked like one, leaning over as though from a great height to catch her words.

"I can understand that," he said thoughtfully. "I suppose it's a matter of finding her identity, her place in relation to all the other things she's going to come up against."

Stephie yawned, sensing that the discussion was turning into one of those dull, incomprehensible adult conversations. Interest waning and milk forgotten, she stirred, feeling cramped and confused, and moved quietly back up the stairs.

In her room, she avoided looking at the dresser, hating her parents for suddenly making her feel ashamed of the horseshoes in her underwear drawer.

She slipped into bed, purposely leaving the door open just in case any more really interesting talk might develop. But she was already asleep when her parents passed her room only a few minutes later as the grandfather clock struck eleven.

"That last log should burn all night, so I left the damper open," her father said. "Remember to close it tomorrow."

"There's no easy way to handle it, Tom," her mother whispered. "She'll just have to get used to the idea."

[14]

## *Chapter two*

BUT SHE DIDN'T GET USED TO IT. THE NEXT DAY IN SCHOOL, shortly after she had told Nancy she could go, she passed him in the hall and they both looked the other way. She hated it . . . this awareness of him that made the school halls a gantlet to be run.

It was funny that she never thought of him as being tall and well-built and good-looking. But, then, he wasn't. He was short and thin and his hair was just hair. She couldn't know yet of his quick, sweet smile or the way his face laughed mostly around the eyes or of the little-boy charm. She thought of him as just . . . him . . . the, a, any old boy who had to be part of the pattern of growing up, as her mother said.

Her mother said it again the Sunday, almost two weeks before the dance, when Stephie was getting ready to go over to Nancy's.

"Just think of him as part of the pattern of growing up." She helped Stephie slip the scarlet dress over her head.

"But why do I have to grow up this Sunday? Next Sunday, Barbara, Jean and Betty can't go tobogganing."

"I think it's very nice of Nancy to have this party

[15]

today so that you will know each other better before the dance."

Stephie jammed her arms into her coat.

"I don't want to get to know him any better. All I want is to get the dance over with."

"Look, Stephie . . ." Edith Rodgers sat down in the satin slipper chair. "Look, Stephie . . ." she said again, looking up and up at the figure of her daughter which seemed to loom over her because the chair was so low.

"I don't feel well, Mother," Stephie said, sagging onto the bed. "I really don't. I think I'm going to . . ."

"No, you're not."

Stephie didn't think so, either, but maybe she could if she really tried. She averted her eyes, afraid her thoughts would show.

"But I really don't feel good, Mother. My stomach is . . ." she trailed off unconvincingly.

Edith Rodgers sat down beside her.

"That's part of it," she said.

"Part of what?" Stephie demanded, struggling to get a moan in her voice.

"The beginning to become adult, grown up. . . ."

"My *stomach* is?"

"Knowing yourself, that you can no longer use a sick stomach or a sore throat to solve your problems. The beginning to become Stephie, become you, that special person that makes you Stephanie Rodgers, not just another amorphous child."

"What's amorphous?"

"Just formless. Uncrystallized. No character."

Stephie got up and walked over to the mirror.

"Who wants character, anyway? I'd rather have Barbara's hair and eyes than character."

Edith Rodgers rose and came over to stand beside Stephie before the mirror.

"You're not Barbara. Barbara's pretty, but you're different. You've got interesting eyes and a lovely, generous mouth. You're different. Be different."

"Different?" Stephie echoed, tears in her voice. "That's the trouble. I am different. Every day. I'm never the same. But Barbara is. Barbara's a size nine. Barbara isn't one size one time and another the next. Barbara doesn't have to buy 'twixt-teen clothes. But I do. I'm always 'twixt something or other."

Her mother's hands gentled on her shoulders.

"Some girls mature faster than others. There isn't any set timetable for it. One day you'll wake up to discover you're not just pretty. That you're attractive in a way that Barbara can never be."

Edith Rodgers saw her lean forward and peer long and searchingly into the mirror.

"Remember to thank Nancy's mother," she reminded her softly.

Stephie swung around, the magic of going-to-be dissipated by the present.

"Remember to tell Daddy to pick me up at five."

"Six thirty," her mother said, forcing compassion out of her voice. "You said it was to last from two to seven. Six thirty's early enough."

"It'll be awful!" Stephie wailed. "I don't want to stay that long!"

[17]

"Six thirty." Her mother gave her a swift hug. "Now hurry or you'll be late."

All the way over, in the scarlet dress and ski suit frame of mind, Stephie fumed. Why did you have to grow up at all? She ran and slid across a small patch of ice in front of Nancy's house. Why, especially, did this growing up business have to start like this . . . with a punch of a bell and Nancy answering it and drawing her in and toward a group around a game table.

"Carol, Bob, Doug, Marge, Scott, Harv," Nancy said. "Stephie, everybody."

Stephie trembled inside. All of them, except Scott, were juniors and seniors. With the easy sureness that comes with being . . . well, seventeen, at least. And being president of the Student Council, and editor of the paper, and chairman of the Prom Committee. All of them smiling at her, Stephie, just a sophomore, just a hall guard, just a third row second seat first soprano.

Stephie smiled stiffly as her eyes slid from face to face. Carol had blonde hair, and Bob had a crew cut, and Doug wore glasses, and Marge sat as if she had a book on her head, and Harv's mouth was shaped like a whistle. And Scott. She couldn't have really described Scott if her life depended on it because she was too embarrassed to do more when introduced than nod at the second stripe in his tie.

It was Harv who twirled an imaginary mustache and exclaimed, "Well, *well!*" He shoved a stack of paper money at her. "Now, honey, you sit right here next to me and let old Uncle Harv show you how the game is played."

[18]

Everyone laughed, Stephie self-consciously, feeling herself blush, and they laughed some more when Marge slid into the chair Harv was indicating and put her arm through his.

"Old Uncle Harv," she informed him, "had better start playing the game."

Everyone laughed again, except Stephie who didn't know whether it was funny or not.

"Stephie knows how to play," Scott blurted. "But I don't. She's got to show me."

Everyone hooted, but it had a friendly sound and Stephie's eyes darted gratefully to Scott's. Why, he's got nice eyes, she thought with surprise, and they make him look as if he's laughing even when he's not. She felt a sort of circus excitement in the pit of her stomach and she looked away in happy confusion.

She couldn't believe it was really six thirty, even with her father standing in the hall talking to Nancy's mother and father. As far as she was concerned, it could have been high noon on a summer day, though she was glad it was dark so her father couldn't see the flush on her face, glad he had walked over instead of driving so that she might attribute the flush to the cold when she got home.

She felt like running but satisfied herself with an occasional skip.

"Cold?" her father asked, breaking his stride to light his pipe.

"No, oh, no!" She cut the excitement out of her voice. "Well, a little."

[19]

"Did you have a good time?"

She wanted to say, yes, yes, yes! Instead she said guardedly, "Oh, it was all right."

"Did you like . . . everybody?"

She nodded.

"I like Scott," her father said. "He's a nice boy."

"I guess so." She took another skip.

Tom Rodgers cleared his throat.

"I know your mother has already talked to you about this. But for what it may be worth, I'd like to tell you about the boy's side of it. He's as scared as you are, you know."

"S-scared?" she echoed, teeth chattering, doubtful that she was simply cold. "Who's scared?"

"Uneasy, then. This may be his first date, too. And one that was arranged for him, not one he asked for."

"Well, I didn't ask for it, either!"

"I know. But some of the responsibility rests on you, also, to make this first date easier and, maybe, good. It's as bad for the boy, Stephie, because he has to make the first move, and it has to be the right one, whether it's a dance step or conversation, or he'll be thought a fool. Sometimes it's difficult to know what's right."

Stephie slowed down.

"I remember when I was a boy," he continued thoughtfully. "I kept all the usual things in my pockets . . . string, old apple cores, pebbles . . . and the usual things in my mind . . . our gang's secret password, how to get out of mowing the lawn, the difference between a Ford and a Chevvy. I never hung up my clothes and rarely combed my hair and hated girls. They were either soft, giggly, and stuck-up or else they were tomboys who could play touch football better than I."

He stopped momentarily and relit his pipe.

"But all of a sudden," he went on, puffing furiously, "all of a sudden I stopped fidgeting and tripping over my shoes in the middle of the floor and found myself riding my bike no hands past a girl's house or cracking my knuckles for her at a party."

"Oh, Daddy!"

"Don't sound so disgusted with your old father," he told her. "I thought it might help to know that boys go through much the same things girls do."

"Doesn't seem you went through so much to me, just showing off."

"Not then. It was later, your age, when I kept my hands in my pockets because I didn't know what to do with them and had other things on my mind, like wanting people to like me and never doing anything right and not understanding girls. They were always saying one thing and meaning another, liking you one day, snubbing you the next."

"Daddy. . . ."

"Yes?"

She kept her eyes on the ground but she knew he had his head cocked toward her in that listening attitude of his.

"Oh . . . nothing. . . ."

He took her hand and walked along swinging it.

"Oh, come on . . . it isn't nothing at all. What were you going to say?"

"Well . . . I was just wondering . . . wondering if if . . . if you remembered your first date."

He chuckled. "I sure do. She had long, fat, yellow curls and she . . ." he checked himself, "and she was beautiful. We went to the movies and I was terrified to hold her hand, afraid she'd get mad if I did, mad if I didn't."

"What did you do?"

"I took a deep breath, grabbed her hand, and held on for dear life. She didn't try to pull away and I was thankful, but then it became embarrassing because my hand began to perspire and I didn't know whether to let it go on perspiring in hers or take it away and maybe have her think that I didn't want to hold her hand." He shook his head. "So you see, boys have their problems, too."

Stephie didn't really see. She thought her father must have been an awfully silly boy. Not at all like Scott who was sure of himself. Scott would never worry about people liking him and understanding girls and holding hands. And Scott would never . . . horrible thing . . . perspire. No. He'd just reach over and seek her hand out gently with his and . . . She caught her breath on the thought.

She ran ahead of her father up the steps to the porch. Maybe this growing up business wasn't so awful, after all.

## ᴇᔈ *Chapter three*

STEPHIE WAS RIGHT. SHE DIDN'T HAVE MUCH FUN IN THE
meantime. Every time she started to, thoughts of the
dance would pop into her head. But strangely enough,
when it came right down to it, she really didn't mind.
She was actually looking forward to the dance.

At times she could hardly contain her excitement.
Everything seemed unreal. Only three days left. She sang
all the time and danced with herself when no one was
looking, and she felt like the movies in which people
danced on stairs and furniture and clouds.

She had seen Scott every day since Nancy's party, in
class, and she had talked to him three times, once when
he had bumped into her in the jam at the door of
Geometry I and said I'm sorry and she said that's all
right, and once when they passed in the halls and he said
hi and she said hi, and yesterday when he stopped her in
the lunchroom and said I'll pick you up at seven thirty
Saturday.

"Seven thirty," Stephie repeated.

He stood in front of her, the thin, dark-eyed face never
quite in repose, jiggling things in his pockets.

Several seconds of nothing passed and she stole a quick
glance at him, but he didn't look as if he was going to

[23]

say anything else. Stephie wondered if he was being polite and waiting for her to make the first move to break away, but how to do it? She couldn't turn her back and walk away. However, she had to do something.

"Seven thirty," she said again, starting the smile and taking one step backwards.

"Mom and Dad are going with the Jensens so I'll have the car," he informed her abruptly.

Anything he said would have halted her, of course, but that really stopped her. A car . . . they were going alone in a car. For some reason she had supposed they'd be going with Nancy and Bob and some of the others. She'd never driven in a car with a boy before.

"I've been driving a long time," he announced, though the slim-shouldered shrug that accompanied it was studiedly offhand. "Six months, at least."

Stephie flushed, wishing he hadn't misinterpreted something she hadn't decided yet was misinterpretation.

"I know."

"You do?"

"I . . . I mean I suppose you're . . . you're a good driver."

His pockets began to tinkle again. People kept coming in and out of the lunchroom and several boys had already made kidding remarks to Scott, so Stephie decided to try it again. She got away with two steps this time.

"What . . . what are you going to wear?" he blurted.

"A dress," she said before she thought, and added, "it's a formal."

"I mean, what color?"

"Pink."

"Pink," he repeated, smiling his quick smile and al-

[24]

ready moving away from her to join a group of boys in the hamburger line. "See you Saturday!"

"Seven thirty," Stephie said for the third time, more to herself than to Scott.

Stephie was glad they had decided on the pink taffeta instead of the blue velveteen. Of course her mother sewed the stole on the strapless top, but Stephie didn't mind, she would have felt uncomfortable without it. It was such a beautiful dress and it stuck out all around and made her look as if she were dancing even when she was standing still.

She tried it on for Barbara the day before the dance. She didn't have to decide whether she liked it, she knew. Immediately. When she looked at herself in the mirror she was unable to control the smile that grew inside her until it broke out all over her face. She didn't need Barbara to tell her that it changed her.

"You're different," Barbara said. "You almost look like a movie star."

Stephie twirled around. Quite gracefully.

"Do I really?"

It didn't require an answer and they both knew it.

"Not just the dress," Barbara said. "You. You act as if you want to go."

Stephie considered and said cautiously, "In a way, yes."

"What way? I thought you said Nancy's party was just all right."

"Well I didn't want to rave about it, especially since you think he's skinny and conceited."

"He is! Oh, I suppose he's all right if you like the thin, dark, jumpy cheerleader type. But he goes around

[25]

with his nose in the air, never paying any attention to . . ." She stopped suddenly and picked up a necklace on the dresser. "Well, was there anything to rave about?"

Stephie adjusted the stole which didn't need any adjustment.

"Not really. But it was kind of fun. It wasn't what I expected." She turned around and faced her. "He's nice," she plunged. "He's not what you think. He's not like all those other boys talking loud and pushing each other around when a girl goes by. He's more . . . more grown up."

The necklace slipped from Barbara's fingers and clattered on the dresser.

"You like him."

Stephie reddened. "I don't know. Not yet. Anyway, my mother's probably right. He's a start."

Barbara sat down on the edge of the bed and stared at her. And Stephie felt a heady sense of power, for the first time with Barbara. Not power, really, a feeling of equality, of confidence in herself. She had dared to contradict her, flatly, willingly, and she had been successful! Barbara's face told her that.

"Want to borrow my necklace, the pink flowered one?" Barbara asked unexpectedly.

Stephie clapped her hands. "Could I? It'd be just the thing!"

She half danced over to Barbara.

"Who are you going with?" Barbara asked, moving over to make room for her on the bed. "Nancy and that crowd?"

Stephie felt some of her confidence ebb.

"No." She almost whispered it. "He's driving."

[26]

"You mean you're going alone? What did your mother say?"

"She wasn't crazy about the idea. But if his father trusts him to drive the car, why shouldn't she?"

Barbara's eyes narrowed.

"Oh, I don't mean that! I mean being alone with him. Aren't you absolutely terrified? He might try to drive with one arm!"

Stephie had thought of it, but as soon as she did she tried to think of something else because she wasn't quite sure whether it was terror or anticipation.

"It could be worse," she told Barbara. "I might have to . . . to sit on his lap if we went with a whole bunch of people."

"I suppose so," Barbara said slowly. Then, "Guess what? I think I'm going out with Mac Anderson next week!"

"No! You mean he asked you for a date?" The word came out easily now.

"Not exactly. But he's sort of been hinting around. Maybe we could double date sometime!"

"Oh, yes!" Stephie hugged her excitedly. "Wouldn't that be fun!"

The grandfather clock started booming and Barbara jumped up.

"That'll be ten," she said. "I said I'd be home at nine thirty. I'll run over with the necklace tomorrow morning and I'll see you Sunday. You can tell me all about it then."

"I will!" Stephie promised, hugging her again. "I will!"

But even as she was saying it, she was wondering. Wondering if there would be anything to tell.

## ◄§ *Chapter four*

SATURDAY CAME, AND WITH IT THE KNOWLEDGE THAT IT had come too soon. Stephie didn't know what on earth had possessed her actually to look forward to it, to think she looked any different, glamorous. Glamorous . . . that hair, those eyes, freckles.

She brushed her hair almost viciously and was perversely glad to see it just hang short and straight as usual.

She stumbled a little in the dress as she reached for the perfume, and caught herself in time, feeling hysteria pushing up through her. Perfume! she thought, not knowing whether it was a laugh or a sob that was going to come out. Could perfume make the funny green of her eyes a mysterious blue?

Where had last night's feeling of confidence gone, the hint of beauty, the sure-footed grace? Now she simply felt gauche, awkward. She was ready a full hour too early, sitting rigidly in the living room, knotted inside and knowing she really could be sick this time without trying at all.

The doorbell rang. She jumped up, sat down, and jumped up again, heart pounding.

"Relax, darling," her mother said. And she smiled at her before she went to the door.

Scott came in looking as strange as she felt, in his dark blue suit, his face whiter than his shirt, clutching a florist's box. He thrust it at Stephie while greeting her mother.

A corsage! Her very first! A mass of tiny flowers nestled deep, deep blue against the green of the florist's waxed paper. She murmured something unintelligible as she fumbled with the corsage. Her hands trembled so that she finally had to turn to her mother.

"It's a bad night out, Scott," her mother said as she pinned the flowers on Stephie's coat.

"It certainly is," Stephie's father agreed, entering the room. "Hello there, Scott."

Scott shook hands with him, and Stephie surprised herself by wishing Scott would make some move to leave before her parents changed their minds.

"You'll be careful, won't you, Scott?" her mother asked, frowning a little.

Scott jammed his hands in his pockets and stared at his feet.

"I'm not driving. My father is. We're riding with my mother and father."

"Well, well!" Tom Rodgers said heartily. "That's fine!"

Stephie didn't know whether she was relieved or disappointed as she watched the frown disappear from her mother's face and something almost like sympathy replace it.

Outside, Stephie looked back and waved before she got in the car.

Inside, she huddled in one corner, Scott in the other. Stephie wished she could think of something to say to

Scott's parents besides yes or no when they tried to address conversation to her. Scott didn't even try. She knew how he must be feeling, telling her that he was going to drive and then having to be driven by his father, but she instinctively knew not to let him know she knew.

It was even worse sitting far apart than close together as they had at the party. It made her more conscious of him than ever. She was certain he felt the same way because occasionally she would catch him looking at her and once she was almost sure he smiled.

And that's how it was, holding thoughts but not hands, all the way to the club where she had a better time dancing with his father. Whenever she danced with Scott her hands became damp and her slippers pink galoshes.

Scott tore his eyes away from his feet.

"You're . . . You're . . ." His voice trailed off but his eyes didn't which was maybe why he forgot to move one of his feet and she stepped on it.

Stephie's face grew pink as she tried and tried to think of some answer. He had opened a conversation. The least she could do was answer. But all she could think of was thank you. So she said it.

"Thank you." A bit hoarsely, but she got it out. The only trouble with it was that she didn't know whether or not what he was going to say was complimentary.

When the number ended and the orchestra tootled for an intermission, they remained on the floor until it was empty. Then they had to move.

"Let's go find some of the others," Scott said, almost dragging her into one of the rooms that opened off the ballroom.

[30]

They were lucky. They spotted Bob almost immediately, carrying a tray full of Cokes to the crowd at the table where Nancy was sitting, when Scott pounded him on the arm.

"What the . . ." Bob started angrily.

Some of the Coke slopped over on his sleeve as he steadied the tray.

"Gosh, I'm sorry." Scott's face reddened as he tried to wipe Bob's sleeve.

"That's all right," Bob muttered in a tone that wasn't all right at all. "Just watch it next time, kid."

Bob started to go, but Scott stepped in front of him.

"You . . . you remember Stephie, don't you?" his voice pleaded.

Stephie smiled brightly.

"Stephie? Oh, yeah. Yeah, sure . . . Hi."

Bob stepped around them.

"Well . . . See you around. . . ."

And there they were, left in the middle of another floor.

"Want a Coke?"

"Well . . . If you want one," Stephie said in a little voice.

"I do if you do."

"Well, I do if you do."

They might never have got the Cokes if Scott hadn't seen Doug up at the Coke bar.

"There's Doug," he said happily. "I'll be right back. You sit here."

He pushed her toward a tiny table.

Stephie sat. Stiffly. For a long time. At least five minutes. Her face felt tight with the smile that never left it.

[31]

She didn't dare let it go because she wanted the couples sitting around her to know she was having a good time. If they ever looked at her.

Scott came back. Alone.

"Where're Doug and Carol?" Stephie asked.

"Oh," airily, "they're with some other people. Said they'd see us later."

"Oh."

Stephie sipped her Coke. She hoped she'd be able to make it last until the orchestra started to play again.

Scott downed his.

"Finished?"

Stephie looked regretfully at her glass, still half-full.

"Oh, yes!"

"Well, let's go. They ought to start playing any minute now."

They took a circuitous route through a lounge and ran smack into Marge and Harv entwined beside a potted palm. Stephie felt the way she did at the movies. Too absorbed to eat her popcorn.

Fortunately, as if on signal, the orchestra started up. Scott and Stephie fairly ran back to the floor.

And that's how the whole evening went. With Scott's cheek surprisingly touching hers when they resumed dancing. A miserably wonderful evening it was.

## ✑§ Chapter five

IT PROGRESSED SLOWLY. AS SLOWLY AS THE STORM COAT that became a yellow slicker and the slicker that became just a sweater slung over her shoulders.

At first, Stephie had wanted to share the wonderful details of that evening with someone, anyone, everyone. She had hugged it to herself for a moment before closing the door on Scott's retreating figure, and then she let it out, this feeling that was like riding a bicycle for the first time or swimming without an inner tube, a Look, Mom! Look at me! feeling. It lasted as long as it took her to clatter half-way up the stairs, and for her mother to snap on the hall light and shush it back down inside her. It stayed there, too, as her mother drew her away from the bedroom where her father lay sleeping, even though she was interested in an I-told-you-so way that Stephie had had a good time. For Stephie found she didn't want to be told so, she wanted to tell it herself. She wanted to tell, not be asked questions about who was there and what did they wear.

Saturday had at long last become Monday as she had wanted it to and didn't want it to by the time it arrived, but Scott was absent Monday, anyway, and two days

[33]

later she got a bad cold and had to stay home. And then it was February and they became 2A's and no longer were in the same geometry class, and before she knew it, Monday had become March and he still hadn't acknowledged her other than as part of the crowd in the halls between classes, let alone asked for another date. Oh, he'd often glance at her during Assembly but then she'd quickly turn her head and pretend interest in the announcement from the stage that the Chess and Checker Club was to meet in Room 801 at three thirty.

Stephie became May-moody . . . Hopeful and despairing . . . flushed and chilled . . . energetic and phlegmatic . . . That's why she was glad that vacation time was almost here and she could go away to Barbara's cottage where she had been invited to spend the summer.

Her mother felt the same way.

"I'll certainly be glad," she said to Stephie's father one evening before dinner, "when school's over and Stephie can get away to Barbara's summer place."

"That bad?" Tom Rodgers asked, opening the refrigerator.

"Quit poking around in there! Dinner will be ready in a minute."

He emerged with a chicken drumstick.

"It must be bad," he commented, perching on the kitchen stool, "when you can't wait to pack her off. What is it this time?"

"This time, any time, the same thing. Scott."

"What about him?"

"He hasn't asked her for another date. Ever since the dance she's been moping around."

"I thought she had a good time at the dance."

"I think she did. She seemed elated enough. Though, if you noticed, the dance marked the beginning of the uncommunicative phase."

"Uncommunicative?"

"She didn't really tell us anything about it. Only that she had a nice time."

He grinned at her.

"What's so funny?"

"You," he said, still grinning. "You wanted to be the modern mother and cut the apron strings in a great big hurry. Why not start thinking of it as a challenge instead of a loss?"

She sank down on one of the kitchen chairs.

"I'm trying, Tom, I really am. But how can I give her real understanding when I can't remember all the things I felt at her age? She's over at Barbara's now, probably telling her all the things she's not telling us."

He got up and kissed the top of her head.

"Things will straighten themselves out."

"I suppose so," she agreed wearily, "all this is just part of this pattern."


Stephie could have told them that as far as patterns went, she'd like to trade hers in on a new one. What seemed like such a good beginning had fizzled out into nothing, absolutely nothing. Well, a pretty good beginning. She couldn't bring herself to tell Barbara everything. She couldn't have described it, anyway, the conversational strain, the physical strain of dancing with him. It was something you just felt, that's all. She had to tell her that he didn't kiss her because she'd asked right out, but, secretly, Stephie was just as glad he hadn't. And there had been good things to tell . . . like the flowers and putting his cheek against hers. It really had been a pretty good beginning.

That's why she couldn't understand his avoiding her. Well, not exactly, he never went out of his way to do it, but acting as if the whole thing had never happened. They were right back where they started except for one thing. They both knew it had happened.

It frightened her more than anything else. Because it might be her own fault. Especially if her father might possibly be right about some of the responsibility being hers to make the date a good one. She hadn't, evidently. She certainly was glad school was nearly over and she could go away to Barbara's cottage.

Glad, that is, until the day Scott unexpectedly walked her home from school.

He had waited for her after her last class. Her voice trembled only a little when she said hi, shyly.

"Hi. Going home?"

"Yes."

"So am I."

They fell into step and Stephie fervently wished she had worn anything else that day but the sickly green sweater which made her eyes look like peeled green grapes. She shifted the books in her arms to hide as much of it as possible, only to have Scott take them from her.

"Only two more days," he said after a block's silence.

"Yes."

"I've got a job."

"Oh."

"At my dad's office."

"Oh."

"So, I'll be around."

"That's . . . nice."

"Maybe," he suggested casually, "we can go swimming or something some time."

"I . . . I can't."

"Why?" Not casual.

Stephie sighed. "I'm going to Barbara's."

"To the lake?"

"For the whole summer."

He kicked at a pebble.

"Gee, that's . . . nice."

"Yes."

They stood uncertainly in front of her house.

"Well . . . See you next September."

He turned to go and Stephie, sick with ineptitude, knew she had to do something about the unimaginable in-betweenness of now and then.

"Scott . . ." It was almost a whisper. She was elated and frightened of her boldness at the same time when she saw him whirl around, the nervous dark eyes dominating the thin face.

"What?" he asked, his lips curving out of little-boy petulance into little-boy charm.

"N-nothing."

"C'mon. You were going to say something." He grabbed her arm as she backed away. "What?"

Stephie took a deep breath and stared at her feet. "Will you . . . write?" She was instantly ashamed for having to ask, but his answer made everything all right.

"Yes. I was going to."

Not maybe, Stephie thought, as she fairly catapulted into the house. Not I don't know or I'll write if you do. But yes . . . I was going to.

And later, in her room, trying to fix her attention upon the next day's assignments, she wondered why, suddenly, everything was so complicated. Why the good things that once, well, just came to her, now had to be coaxed. Why she was suddenly filled with all sorts of funny feelings, baffling because they were unknown and had no names to be looked up.

At the lake, Stephie wrote to her mother. About games and sunburn and food, though she really would have liked to write about stars and moonlight and shadows on a forest trail but was embarrassed to do so. Stephie received letters, too. But the ones that meant the most were those from Scott which were painfully brief and hinted at everything and then in parentheses ha-ha'd it away to nothing. It was an unendurably long summer.

When Barbara's mother suggested that they might invite two boys of their choice up for a week-end, the girls were ecstatic. Stephie immediately wrote her mother and asked her to contact Scott's mother. And it was arranged for the following Saturday and Sunday.

Stephie never wished now that she had Barbara's red hair and uninhibited vivacity. Which was good. Because Scott was coming to see Stephie with her short straight hair and softening angularity and just-turned-sixteen diffidence. And that was the way he found her when he got there with Mac, Barbara's friend.

Mac was one of those nice persons who are never described as being tall or short or in-between, or athletic or smart or funny, but merely as somebody's friend.

You certainly could tell Mac was crazy about Barbara, Stephie thought, as she watched Scott chasing her down the beach for throwing a handful of sand at him. It wasn't just his eyes that waited on her, it was in his walk, a behind kind of walk which never quite brought him up beside her, and in the way he cocked his head to listen to her screeches as Scott dragged her into the water and ducked her.

Stephie sat uneasily on the sand beside Mac and wished the other two would come back so she wouldn't have to be alone with him. She finally turned on the portable radio.

"It sure is nice up here," Mac ventured, reluctantly taking his eyes off the distant figure of Barbara.

"I've been coming here for years. And spring vacations and other times, we go to my grandfather's farm," she said, so quickly her words overlapped his. She wished she had spaced them more so that they would have taken up more time.

Somebody loudly started selling cars and Stephie switched to another station.

"Barbara tell you about the November hay ride the Hi Y's are giving?" And with pronouncement of the name his eyes swung back to the two splashing in the shallows.

"No."

"I guess she hasn't had time," he said, eyes straining again to the water's edge. He looked abashed. "I mean, she hasn't had time because I just asked her myself. She said maybe you and Scott would go, too."

[39]

"I . . . I don't know. Maybe. . . ."

And her own eyes followed his to the two figures now wrestling on the shoreline. If she were Barbara, she thought regretfully, she could ask Scott to go. Barbara wouldn't think anything of it.

No, Barbara would never mind asking him, particularly since Stephie was sure she'd changed her mind about not liking Scott. She had a feeling that Barbara didn't think he was conceited any more, now that she knew him better. And thin, maybe, but not skinny. It made Stephie feel good. Bird-soaring good. Because it would be awful if a Best Friend didn't like the same things you liked. Especially things that really mattered.

She sighed and wished again that she could ask him. But she wasn't Barbara, she was Stephie, and she was glad she was Stephie. Because that's who Scott came up there to find, not Barbara who laughed and played easily and whose red hair clung curly to her head like a poodle's, even in the water.

So Scott found Stephie to be Stephie in the water with her hair plastered to her head, scrambling over the trails and looking as if she were sort of growing out of herself, and on a sand dune at night staring fixedly up, down, or anywhere but at Scott seated close beside her.

"It's beautiful, isn't it?" she asked brightly.

Scott clumsily slid his arm around her.

"What is?"

"Oh . . ." Stephie caught her breath and gestured vaguely. "Oh . . . oh, the water and sky and everything."

With his other hand, he caught hers and held it.

"I . . . I can think of nicer things."

[40]

Stephie was afraid to ask him what for fear he'd tell her and she wouldn't know what to answer.

"Look at me," he said, the command almost ending in a squeak.

Stephie hung her head.

"I won't . . . I won't hurt you," he added, releasing her hand and turning her head gently toward him.

As he slowly bent his head, the intensity of his stare held her even more than his hands which drew her closer. Stephie began to thump inside and knew she could never bring herself to do anything to stop it. She just wished, wildly, that he'd get it over with.

"You smell good," he blurted almost against her lips. "Like bread."

And then he kissed her, softly and lingeringly, and the thumping became a whooshing, and Stephie knew why they never meant it in the movies when they slapped their faces, it was awfully silly, the slapping, that is, and she wished the kiss would never end.

When he at last raised his head, they looked at each other wonderingly, and the silence was beautiful and right.

It was Stephie who finally broke it.

"Thank you," she said gravely.

But she was smiling inside. Her mother was right . . . in a way. The first time wasn't easy. Like falling off a bicycle or belly-flopping from a diving board. The first time wasn't easy at all. For anything. But there were some first times, Stephie guessed, like this one, when you wished that there didn't have to be a second time or a third time. Just a first time.

[41]

*ea§ Chapter six*

YOU COULDN'T REALLY TELL BY LOOKING THAT IT HAD happened. The thermometer still read in the upper eighties and everything was still that heavy green and people still rode around in convertibles with the tops down. It could have been summer instead of September. But for the air. But for the indescribable something in the air that made people start thinking about rakes and mulching and broken glass to be replaced in storm windows.

September. Stephie never really liked September. It always sort of sneaked up and caught you with your sweaters down at the bottom of the cedar chest. It meant school and, more particularly, Science, which Stephie hated, and silly old boys.

But this year, her junior year, was different. It meant a size thirty-four pullover instead of a thirty-two. It meant a course in French Romantic Plays. It meant Scott, who had given her her first kiss without benefit of spinning bottles, flashlights or closet post-offices.

Stephie glanced out the bedroom window. The day had an overripe warmth to it that she sensed rather than felt as she turned away and began brushing her hair. Her hands were cold when she tried to pat the sides into some semblance of a wave, but for all her effort it still hung down short and straight.

Stephie was beginning to wonder if this first day back was going to be as wonderful as she had anticipated. Maybe he wouldn't remember. After all, almost a whole month had passed since he and Mac had come up for the week-end at Barbara's cottage.

Stephie leaned closer toward the mirror. She shivered and jerked around as though she could run away from the freckles and wide mouth and strange green eyes. No . . . Scott wouldn't remember in September sunlight what he had seen by August moonlight . . . Scott. . . .

Stephie looked at the clock. She had plenty of time so she grabbed her sweater and ran down the stairs and most of the way to school. Up to within a block of it, when her eyes ran on and found him in a group on the corner and her feet almost stopped moving. She was out of breath. Half a block and minutes later, she was still out of breath.

"Stephie! Wait for me, Stephie!"

Stephie turned. She was glad to be able to turn and stop.

"I never thought I'd catch up with you!" Barbara was a little out of breath herself. "What's the rush?"

Stephie was still breathing hard. "I . . . I thought I was late."

Barbara caught up a straggling strand of red hair with a bobby pin.

"You sound . . . Hey, there's Scott! Oh, Scott! Scott!"

Stephie tried to intercept Barbara's wave. "No, don't," she begged, feeling the flush crawl up her face.

Barbara turned and looked at her with a darting something in her eyes that made Stephie wonder if Barbara were beyond the stage of jumping up and down and clapping her hands and chanting, "Stephie loves Scott, Stephie loves Scott, Stephie loves Scott!"

She was beyond it, but not much, because she called Scott's name again. Louder this time. Then said, "He's seen us, anyway, and he heard me the first time, so c'mon."

He hadn't, of course, but with the eyes of the group now focused on them, Stephie had to keep up with her or appear to be dragged.

Scott left the group and came up to them and Barbara gave him a little push and smiled pertly, and Stephie wished that she, too, could kid around and be natural instead of standing there awkwardly.

Scott smiled at Barbara and pushed her back.

"Run along, little one. Mac's waiting for you over there."

Barbara sort of squeaked, gave him another push, and ran before he could catch her.

Scott laughed and turned back to Stephie.

"She's a cute kid."

Stephie had to agree. Besides, it was true.

"Hope she runs into Mac.

"But you said. . . ."

He grinned a little-boy grin. "I made that up. I wanted to see you alone."

Stephie began to run again, inside.

[44]

"You . . . you did?"

"Yes. I thought we'd . . . I thought maybe you'd like to go to a show Saturday."

"Saturday?"

"Oh. You have another date."

"No! Oh, no! No, I don't!" she said quickly, thinking how surprising it was that he thought she had another date. And wondering if she had seemed too eager, she added. "That is . . ." and stopped, then rushed on because she didn't care, she was so glad, "I'd love to go."

"It's a date, then. I'll pick you up about eight."

Stephie nodded, a little dazed, hearing the bell ring for the first class as though from a great distance.

He walked up the steps beside her into the building and Stephie was glad the halls were dark because she didn't want him to see the smile that just wouldn't go away. If she wasn't pretty, maybe her mother was right about character. Whatever this character business was, it was all right.

About eight came and went and became exactly eight forty-seven before he picked her up in his father's car.

Stephie talked. And talked and talked. She couldn't help it. After the long silent minutes of sitting and waiting and pacing and waiting and looking and waiting she just couldn't seem to stop.

"And Barbara called," she was saying, "and said you were over there and she. . . ."

"I just stopped to give. . . ."

"Oh, that was all right." She bit her lip. "You don't have to make any excuses. I mean you don't have to tell me why you were there. It's just that this cousin of her's

[45]

is in town, Bill, I think she called him, and Mac and some other people were coming over and she wanted me to meet him, this cousin of hers, I mean. . . ."

"Bill."

"Yes, that's his name, Bill," she agreed feverishly, knowing this was going all wrong for some strange reason. "And I said of course our date wasn't really definite, but I'd. . . ."

"Wasn't it?"

"Well, you said maybe Saturday we could go to a show."

"I didn't say 'maybe' that way and you know it!"

"Well, it got so late. . . ."

"I tried to tell you why I was. . . ."

"Oh, it's really not necessary," she said gaily. "It really doesn't matter at all. It's just. . . ." She stopped. "Why are we parking?"

"We're here." Flatly.

"Where?"

"Barbara's. She told me to bring you back."

"She. . . ."

"I thought the two of you had it all settled," he said grimly. "Don't you want to go?"

Stephie tried to smile. "If . . . if you want to."

"I do. I wouldn't want you to miss meeting Bill."

Stephie opened her mouth and at last it came out, frightened. "Scott. . . ."

But he didn't hear her. He was already out of the car and walking around to open the door for her.

She couldn't do anything but get out and walk beside him silently up to the door.

Inside, it wasn't any better. Oh, it was gay enough,

with Bill and the others, but not with Scott. He talked to her occasionally, but it was had-to talk not want-to talk as he gave Barbara. Stephie was sure they'd leave early. She wanted to. But they didn't go, even when most of the others had gone. In fact, they were the last to leave.

Stephie hoped when they got out to the car that Scott might drive around for a bit and say something, anything, to wipe out all the awfulness of the evening. But he didn't. And when she saw him drive straight ahead and swing the car into the curb in front of her house, she felt with a terrible certainty that it was finished. That's why she wasn't prepared for the action that left her feeling like all the times she had sat and sat only to have the photographer come out from under his hood without clicking the shutter.

He shook his hands off the wheel, reached over and shoved her back on the seat, and then leaned back himself and stared at her.

Stephie squirmed a little.

"I . . . I had a lovely time."

"Did you? I didn't."

She wet her lips.

"But you insisted we. . . ."

"You already had it all fixed."

"I didn't! You were late and I thought you weren't coming and. . . ."

"Mac's mother told me he was at Barbara's so I stopped to return a math book of his. I tried to tell you but you wouldn't listen."

"I . . . I didn't know. We just . . . just got all mixed up."

[47]

"Well, there's one thing we're not going to get all mixed up. That we're going to get straight right now."

He shifted his position but he didn't touch her.

"You're not Bill's girl," he continued, staring straight ahead out the windshield. "You're not any of those guys' girl who were there tonight. You're . . ." His voice faltered and he cleared his throat. "You're . . . you're my girl." The last was almost a whisper, but Stephie would have heard it even if he hadn't said it.

She watched, heart pounding in the silence, his hands clench the wheel.

"Say it," he said, his eyes still fixed on the windshield.

She started to. "I'm . . ." and stopped, embarrassed, willing him to pretend she had said it.

But he didn't help her and she had to try to finish it. "I'm . . . I'm your . . . your . . ." Her voice trailed off.

"What?" he insisted.

"Girl." She sighed the word and hoped it was enough.

It was. Because he turned from the windshield toward her and she thought now, now, here it comes, just like last August, only better, because this kiss would be serious. And she thought, half closing her eyes, that she didn't have to try to remember last August any more.

It was fortunate that her eyes were only half-closed, because she saw that he still sat where he was, motionless, a smile edging his mouth.

And the strangest part of all was that she didn't feel cheated but rather sort of glad . . . in a way. When Scott took her to the door, she didn't wonder if he'd ask to see her again, and she didn't mind when he didn't.

[48]

They stood there for a moment saying nothing, smiling at each other, and then he put out his hand and she laid hers in it, and then he turned and ran back down to the car.

When she closed the door, she leaned against it briefly and thought that surely her first kiss in August had nothing on shaking hands in September.

Stephie loved school this year. There were Coke dates in September. There was a school dance in October. And there was Civics. She liked Civics best because it came last and then she could stop by Bronson's Drugstore and maybe bump into Scott. Everything was wonderful. Everything was turning out fine. Just as when she used to write

Stephanie Rodgers

and below it

Scott Parker

and strike out the same letters in each name, s's, o's, p's, e's and r's, and count the remaining ones like buttons—hate, courtship, love, friendship, marriage. It always came out love. When she used her full name, that is. She never used Stephie because that always ended in friendship. Scott Parker . . . Stephanie Parker. . . .

She felt a great surging, arms-flung-wide happiness. And she didn't care who knew it. Even her mother. They were riding downtown on the bus to keep Stephie's dental appointment and then go shopping.

"Mother," she said suddenly, "were you ever in love? I don't mean with Daddy. I mean really in love."

Edith Rodgers glanced quickly around and knew that

[49]

the man across the aisle wasn't smiling at anything he was reading on the sports page.

"Not so loud!"

"Well, were you or weren't you?" Stephie stage whispered.

"Of course! But this is no place to discuss it."

She tried to read, but Stephie's question kept intruding. Forty minutes and two chapters later, she knew she'd have to read them all over again.

"Hurry!" she told Stephie, "or we'll be late for your appointment!"

Stephie loitered for a moment in front of a department store window frothing with languishing lingerie.

"What was he like?"

Edith Rodgers didn't pretend she didn't know to whom she was referring. She told her.

"He was as unprepossessing as all boys are whom girls your age think they're in love with until they grow up and meet a man like your father and learn what love really is!" and was instantly sorry she said it.

Stephie didn't say anything. Her face wore a closed-up look as she turned into the dental building.

Her mother gave her a bright begging smile.

"I'm having lunch with your father," she said hurriedly, "but I'll be back by two to get you and then we'll go shopping. I know we'll find some lovely things."

Stephie didn't answer. Just nodded a tight little nod and walked away.


But her mother couldn't dampen Stephie's happiness for long. There were the Coke dates and the school dance and there were the telephone calls. Telephone calls were even better than dates, in a way. You could half-way say things you could never half say when he was not only listening but looking at you.

She didn't talk. She breathed conversation.

"Oh, you know what."

She cradled the phone like the stuffed bear she used to sleep with.

"Well, I'm always saying it. You say it."

She giggled.

"Not that! I'm supposed to say that! You're supposed to say. . . ."

She turned on her other side.

"I'm . . . I'm glad you are."

She rolled over and saw her mother standing in the doorway making motions.

"Well, I can't shout it. Dinner's ready."

She stood up.

"I do, too."

She giggled again.

"Not me . . .," whispering . . ., "you."

Her mother returned to the doorway.

"Yes. See you tomorrow. . . ."

And tomorrow came. And went. And miraculously another tomorrow. And another. And soon she didn't have to fear them any more because they became just like another today.

## ❦ *Chapter seven*

AT FIRST GOING STEADY WAS A ONCE IN A WHILE THING. When Stephie and Scott dated, they dated only each other. But in recent weeks once in a while had become all the time. Stephie now wore Scott's ring on a chain around her neck. She walked with him to and from school. She met him before each class. She talked with him nightly on the telephone. They held hands openly and without embarrassment. She was going steady.

That's why the hay ride was such fun. Because she wasn't with a boy she didn't like and so didn't have to worry about his putting his arm around her. And she didn't have to worry about the barn part where they stopped for cider and doughnuts and dancing, worry about whether they would ever change partners or have to dance and dance and dance with each other the whole time or else pretend an inordinate thirst or hunger.

This way was so much better. When they danced together it was easy and good, not conscious of each other as each other but as part of themselves. She supposed it was this sureness of Scott, a sureness that came from many dates and many conversations, that made even hand-holding a natural, enjoyable thing, not as it was at first when, hand in hand you could only sustain that high awareness so long before that electrifying something became uncomfortable.

She was happy about the sureness, too, because it made her sure of herself, made being with other boys, when on rare occasions they traded dances, not something to be feared, but enjoyed. For the first time she was able to relax and not be afraid she couldn't make the light, easy comment. Like now, with Mac, while Scott danced with Barbara.

"Scott's lucky," Mac said, bringing two glasses of cider outside to the fence railing on which Stephie perched. "He knows where he stands."

"Heart on my sleeve, you mean?" she asked with a little smile.

Mac smiled back. "Not on your sleeve. Here." He poked a finger at the base of her throat. "It jumps up here and pounds away. I know. I've watched you."

"I don't want it to be that much of a give-away."

He downed his cider and lifted himself up beside her. "That's another reason why Scott's lucky."

"What is?"

"The way you are. Right to the point. No beating around the bush like most girls. You don't get flustered and act as if you don't know what I'm talking about when I say you like him. You come right out and admit it."

They sat for a moment listening to the music and watching couples dance by the open doorway.

"That's why," he at last continued somewhat hesitantly, "I didn't think you'd mind my asking you something. You don't have to answer if you don't want to."

[53]

"All right," Stephie agreed.

"Well . . ." He looked away in embarrassment. "I thought maybe you'd tell me . . . I mean . . . Well just how did Scott ask you to go steady?" He turned to face her now that it was out.

"He didn't do anything, he didn't say anything," she told him.

Mac's face was as perplexed as his voice.

"Nothing? He said nothing?"

"He never actually put it in words," she explained. "He never said let's go steady or how about going steady or anything like that."

Mac still looked confused.

"Oh, he once told me a long time ago, two or three months ago, anyway," she calculated swiftly, "that I was his . . . his girl, but he never said anything about going steady."

"I've been going with Barbara that long," he said wistfully, "but nothing happens. I . . . I asked her to go steady and she sort of laughed, and I thought maybe I didn't go about it right. Sometimes," he added as though talking to himself, "sometimes she acts as though she likes me and then . . ." His voice lost its dreamy quality. "But then, you know how she is," he finished lamely.

"Yes," Stephie breathed. If anyone did, she did.

Mac's eyes darted over to hers as though he just remembered he was talking to Barbara's Best Friend.

"I'm not griping, understand," he said anxiously. "I'd rather have it this way than no way."

"I know," she said softly.

And she really did. And what she didn't know and didn't imagine, Barbara had told her. Just last week, in fact.

"Why don't you give Mac a break?" Stephie had dared to ask.

"What for?"

Stephie was surprised at the genuine surprise in Barbara's voice.

"Because . . . because he's nice, that's why. And he's crazy about you. And I think you must like him a little because you go out with him as much as anybody else."

Barbara resumed tucking prom bids around her mirror.

"I go out with a lot of people I don't like. This one, for instance." She reached up and took down a tiny suede square embossed with crossed sabers. "Remember? I told you about it. He was simply repulsive . . . But isn't the bid cute? I'd never been to a military ball before."

Stephie handed it back to her.

"Why go with Mac at all, then? You'd be doing him a favor."

Barbara was now sitting cross-legged on the floor, sorting through a jumble of snapshots. She looked up.

"Mac? You're kidding!" She poked in the pile. "You know he'd simply be lost if I wasn't around to give him a pat once in a while," she said, her red head bobbing emphatically.

Stephie, knowing it to be true, sat silent.

"Here!" Barbara carolled then. "I knew it was here somewhere. That picture we took at the lake this summer. I've been meaning to give it to Scott."

Stephie accepted the proferred snapshot. She couldn't help it. She gasped.

"You wouldn't!"

"Why not? He said he wants it."

"But look at it!" And knew while she was saying it

[55]

that she shouldn't be making something big of it because Barbara unfailingly would make it bigger in some way.

Barbara got up and looked over her shoulder.

"It's good of Scott and Mac is heeling beside me beautifully. I suppose I should have combed my hair, but I've taken worse pictures."

If she had, Stephie hadn't seen them. Barbara looked as she always looked, pixie-piquant and momentarily butterfly-still. Stephie stared at herself and saw, though she knew it was the crazy angle from which the picture was taken, what she had always felt—the stumbling, fumbling, awkward bigness next to Barbara. She knew she was only an inch taller and three pounds heavier, but it didn't make any difference. If you felt big, you were big.

"And it looks just like you," Barbara pointed out.

It was too late to pretend disinterest in the picture, and though she wanted to tear it up right there and then, she forced herself to toss it casually on the night table.

"That's all right," Barbara said slyly. "You can have it. I found the negative, too."

Stephie didn't rise to the bait. She walked over to the mirror and studied the dance bids.

"I don't know how you can do it, going out with boys you don't like. Like Mac."

"I don't hate him. Besides, he's handy to go places with whenever nobody I like has asked me. Most of the boys I like are already taken . . . like Scott. You're lucky."

Stephie warmed to the subject of Scott as she always did.

"I know," she said earnestly, forgiving Barbara about the snapshot, feeling sympathy course through her. She couldn't imagine ever feeling sorry for Barbara, and she

[56]

couldn't understand it, but she did. She said, "He is wonderful, isn't he?"

She crossed to Barbara swiftly and put an arm around her.

"But you could be just as lucky if you gave a boy half a chance."

Barbara gave her a long full look and there was a miserable mixed-up something in her eyes that made Stephie want to look any place else but at them, in them.

"I'd like to, I really would. But when I go somewhere with someone I always see somebody else I'd rather talk to and dance with and, you know, just fool around with."

And though she still looked at her, Stephie couldn't see anything in Barbara's eyes any more.

"Scott's a lot like me," she went on. " He likes to mix at parties, kid around."

"I know," Stephie said. "That's what makes going out with him such fun. He makes everybody have a good time."

"Not Mac. He stands around saying nothing, doing nothing, just waiting to catch my eye and smile that trembly smile."

"He would if you came back once in a while and talked to him or something."

"I can't come back," Barbara said cryptically, "because I was never there in the first place."

Which really wasn't so cryptic, the more you thought about it, Stephie had concluded.

Mac waved his hand in front of her face, bringing her back to the fence railing and the sounds of a square dance now beginning inside the barn.

[57]

"A penny for your thoughts."

She smiled at him and shook her head.

"Some things, Mac, don't have to be put into words. Like going steady. Words don't make it happen."

"You make it sound so easy. . . ."

It was easy, Stephie thought later, jouncing along in the wagon snuggled into the curve of Scott's arm. At least if you were Scott and Stephie. Why she almost had to squeeze her eyes tight shut and struggle to remember how it had been . . . everything skittering around inside her, every thought, every emotion sharply edged. All she was conscious of now was the wish that everybody could be as contented as she. All the time.

All the time even included that spent away from Scott. At home, for instance, with her parents. Her mother, she knew, didn't approve of her going steady, but she didn't say anything right out about it. Once she came pretty close to it.

"Why don't you ever go out with other boys occasionally?" she asked.

Stephie shrugged and continued leafing through a magazine. "They never ask me."

"Maybe you don't give them a chance," she suggested so casually that Stephie knew it wasn't casual at all.

And Edith Rodgers, seeing the defensive look on her daughter's face as she tossed the magazine aside, went on quickly.

"I mean, Scott's nice, really nice, I like him a lot, he's always welcome here, you know that. But sometimes dating others will give you a new perspective . . . of Scott . . . make you appreciate his nice qualities even more."

"I already know how nice he is."
And there wasn't any answer to that.

"She's going steady," Edith Rodgers announced dolefully one Saturday evening after dinner, bringing the coffee into the living room.

"Um," Tom Rodgers said behind the paper.

"Did you hear what I said?"

He put the paper aside. "For heaven's sake, Edith, just wait it out. Forbid something and you know it becomes more alluring."

"I know. But she's missing out on so much."

"Maybe not as much as you think, since going steady seems to be the thing to do now."

"But why do they all have to act in a herd and do what everyone else does?"

He reached for her hand.

"Look," he said gently. "I know Scott sometimes is brash and cocky, but there comes a time when Stephie has to make her own mistakes."

"And suffer the consequences?"

"Yes. Maybe Scott will be one, I don't know. But all we can do is wait. Everything will turn out all right. Just you wait and see."

So Stephie was contented even at home, because after that once her mother never referred to going steady again. Deep down she knew it was some sort of compromise on her mother's part, but it was easy almost to convince herself that her mother now approved or had at least resigned herself to it. Easy because of the way her mother acted. Respecting her ideas and opinions even when they differed. Easy because of the way she acted with Scott. Her father, too. Setting another place for him at the dinner table. Letting him borrow the car when Mr. Parker's was being repaired. There was a little restraint, a watchfulness, a guarded enthusiasm, but it was almost as good as a whole-hearted, voiced acceptance. Stephie imagined that things really couldn't be much better than they already were, what with the wonderful, intimate, homely feeling she got as she heard her mother laugh at something he said, watched her father teach him to play chess while she slowly turned as her mother pinned up the hem of a formal to ballerina length, saw them both respond to the expressive little-boy smile. It was just that sometimes she couldn't help longing for a complete acceptance, which would surely come like Christmas or being seventeen instead of sixteen or any other sure thing. But waiting was a little worrisome, because some time Scott might not say anything funny enough to evoke a laugh or he might make a really stupid move like opening Queen's pawn to Queen's four.

But most of the time she was contented enough with the way things were, feeling herself succumbing, week by week, to the wonder of wonderful parents. Succumbing to the discovery that parents could be friends. Not Best Friends, maybe, but you could actually like them, not just love them. The new relationship with her mother was best of all because her mother's acceptance now made it possible for her to make girl-talk, Scott-talk, cup-of-tea-talk with her.

Once Scott even kissed her good night in front of her parents and they didn't look even a little bit startled. It was just on the cheek, but she thought that this is how being married must feel, calm and comfortable and sort of . . . sort of benign.

It was particularly comfortable whenever the phone rang and she didn't have to rush and half stumble to it, hoping, hoping it would be him only to have it go leaden in her hand as the voice said Mrs. Rodgers, please.

She was sprawled one afternoon, stomach down, on the couch reading, when the phone rang for the third time before she finally stirred to answer it.

She kept her thumb in the book to hold her place as she picked up the receiver.

"H'lo."

She crumpled up on the library couch.

"Oh. Hi."

She brought up her knees so that the book rested on them.

"Nothing. Just reading."

She opened the book.

"Hm?"

She looked reluctantly at the page number and closed the cover.

"Yes, I'm here. No. No, I didn't forget. Did you get the bid yet? What's it like?"

She shook off her shoes.

"Um . . . Yes, I hear you."

She sat up and began scrunching into her shoes.

"Golly, if you called just to argue. . . ."

She stood up.

"Well . . . you certainly sounded like. . . ."

She sat down again.

"I know . . . There's more to these things than . . ." she half smiled.

"Me, too . . . I didn't mean to. . . ."

She nodded.

"Hm . . . Yes . . . All right . . . Eight thirty . . . 'Bye."

She stopped in the kitchen to get a glass of milk.

"Don't spoil your dinner," her mother said. "Who was that?"

"Scott. About the dance Saturday. He's on some committee or other."

"Scott?" Her mother looked up from the salad bowl to the clock on the wall. "Why, you were only on the phone ten minutes."

She drank the milk. "Was I?"

"Will you set the table, please, and put one of those mats under the potatoes . . . It's usually at least an hour."

Stephie opened a cabinet door.

"Well, there was nothing much to talk about. Just what time he's going to pick me up."

Her mother looked at her for a minute and then turned back to the salad bowl.

"What are you going to wear?"

"I don't know. The blue, I guess."

"Didn't you wear that the last time?"

Stephie poked around for the silverware.

"Yes. But Scott's seen them all. And besides, I've only got three."

Her mother looked over at her again, frowning a little.

"Is this a special affair? Do you want a new dress?"

"Oh, no, Mom! It's only a Christmas dance." She smiled at her over her shoulder as she carried the dishes into the dining room. "Anyway, Scott likes the blue."

But setting the table, Stephie paused for a moment to wonder, herself, at the brevity of her telephone conversation. But only for a moment.

[62]

## ᦂ Chapter eight

INSTEAD, STEPHIE WORE THE RED TAFFETA SATURDAY THAT
sort of flickered when she moved. She pinned the sprigs
of mistletoe which Scott brought her to her waist. Two
hours later, seated before the fireplace in the heavily
carved and upholstered room off the dance floor, she was
thinking how fresh they had stayed. Nothing remarkable
about that, since she had danced only twice, and then
one could hardly call that dancing, stopping as they did
every few minutes to confer about bid receipts and
whether the tap dancer and baritone had arrived yet for
the entertainment.

Stephie glanced through the archway and saw Scott
in yet another conference with the band leader. She then
watched him bend over the blonde singer whose appear-
ance belied her prim posture, and saw his words blend
into the winning smile. Something about the scene
bothered her, but before she could decide what it was
the music started up once more. Stephie tapped her foot
impatiently.

"Scott need an excuse?"

She looked around and up to see Jim Stuart, hands in
pockets, leaning against the fireplace, his shoulders

hunched up in the suit as though it were a football jersey. Jim looked like the football player he was. That's all Stephie ever thought of him as being whenever she passed him in the halls in school. Maybe that's why she was a little startled when he suddenly became Jim Stuart.

"Excuse for what?" she asked.

His eyes strayed to the mistletoe at her waist and Stephie, annoyed, felt herself blush.

He looked strangely flustered. "Forget it. It's none of my business. It just seemed like a bright way to open a conversation."

Stephie regarded him frankly, the sandy hair, the gray eyes, the straight mouth that didn't curve into a smile, but, rather, angled into one, which wasn't often because it wasn't the kind of mouth that smiled just to be doing something.

"That's all right," Stephie said shyly.

They stared at each other in the uneasy silence.

"I'm not the kind to poach on someone else's property . . . But where's the ball and chain?" he asked abruptly, gesturing toward the single strand of pearls around her neck.

Stephie's hand flew to her throat and she felt the flush crawl up under her fingers. She didn't explain that she hadn't worn the chain with Scott's ring because the pearls looked better with her dress.

She didn't answer at all, abruptly annoyed. Annoyed with herself for feeling strangely flattered and annoyed with Jim for making her feel that way. Why should Jim suddenly pick on her after years of not noticing her at all? She thought the answer came to her when she looked

[64]

around for Jim's date and found her, the upper half of her, over in a corner in the middle of a circle of suits.

"What's the matter," she finally inquired tartly, "can't you take competition?"

Jim eyes followed hers.

"Not when it's sought . . . That was a low blow," he said softly. "I came over here to talk to you because I wanted to. No other reason."

He was sincere and she knew it. "I'm sorry," she said contritely.

Though he hadn't moved from the fireplace, Stephie felt as though he were leaning over her.

"You haven't answered my question. You're not the evasive type."

Scott answered it instead. He came up behind Stephie and half sat on the back of the sofa.

"What're you doing with my girl, Stuart?"

His voice was amiable, but his hands on her bare shoulders weren't.

Jim straightened slowly, taking his hands out of his pockets.

"Nothing. Unfortunately."

He smiled briefly and moved away to join his date.

Scott jerked to his feet.

"What kind of a crack was that?"

"Crack?" Stephie rose leisurely and began walking back to the dance floor. "No crack."

"Well, it sounded like one to me." He grabbed her arm and spun her around to face him. "What did you two talk about?"

"Nothing."

"Unfortunately?"

"Unfortunately?"

"Yes, unfortunately. Nothing unfortunately. That's what he said, didn't he?"

"Oh, Scott. . . ."

"Oh, Scott, nothing! Did you tell him you were my girl?"

"I didn't have to," she snapped. "You took care of that."

He took her in his arms and danced her into a corner.

"I didn't know you were the type who went for football players."

"Oh, for heaven's sake, Scott! We've both known Jim ever since we were freshmen. Since when is it a crime to talk to somebody we've known for years?"

"Okay, okay. So he hasn't traveled in our crowd, but there's always a first time, and I didn't think you were the type. . . ."

"Type?" she repeated angrily. "I'm not a type! I'm me! Stephie!"

His arm tightened around her waist.

"You're my Stephie."

She sighed and softened in his embrace.

"That's better," he whispered.

They continued dancing in and out of the corner.

Then, "What did you talk about?"

She stiffened slightly.

"Nothing, really, Scott. . . ."

"What was he trying to do?"

She shrugged as much as the music would permit.

"Oh, I don't know . . . Just keeping me company, I guess. He saw me sitting alone and. . . ."

[66]

"Sure, trying to cut in on. . . ."

"No," she interrupted quickly. "And it was nice," she added sharply, "having some attention given me."

"Meaning?"

"Meaning that it's been a long time since you've noticed anything about me!"

"I didn't know I was supposed to mention things all the time! I thought you knew. You should know."

"I would if I heard them as often as the other girls you hover over! Like Barbara! Or . . . that . . . that stage-whispering vocalist with the band tonight!"

Scott's laugh came off this time, low, but exultant, and Stephie felt a little sick because she knew right then what had bothered her about the scene she had witnessed earlier. She hadn't minded. Now, half-panicked because she hadn't, she realized that she had given Scott the impression of jealousy when all it really was was a resentful striking back at him and his belittling attitude toward Jim.

She tried to push down her anger because she knew she had to pretend something she knew to be otherwise. But it was different, wasn't it, when there was a good reason behind the pretense . . . like not wanting to hurt someone you cared about when you couldn't possibly explain the involved why of not being jealous? Stephie prayed that Scott wouldn't ask what she knew he was going to ask, but he did. So she had to do what she knew she was going to have to do, anyway.

"Jealous?"

She forced herself to thrust out her chin and toss her head to make the answer less believable.

"No."

[67]

She could tell by his pleased expression that it worked. He thought she was, but she wasn't. And it wasn't because she cared any less. It was because she knew that Scott, down deep, liked only her. And she felt ashamed of herself that she had betrayed that feeling when Jim questioned her about Scott's ring. Why, Scott's display of jealousy was a sign of the immaturity she now recognized in herself when she reacted to Jim the way she did.

And suddenly it came to her. If she recognized that immaturity in herself, that meant she had grown up, didn't it? She smiled. Grown up . . . It might take Scott a little longer to catch up, but then everyone said that boys always take longer than girls.

Scott gave her a quick little squeeze and brushed his lips across her cheek. She smiled again and at last rested rhythmically in his arms.

She didn't wonder why she didn't respond wildly to his gesture of affection, as she had wondered a few days ago about her response to his voice on the phone. She knew. She accepted it. If the act of talking or holding hands or kissing had lost its tumultuousness, well, that was all right. The feeling had been replaced by one that was saner and more mature. Stephie didn't care. It was just part of being adult.

*✑§ Chapter nine*

THE CHRISTMAS TREE CAME DOWN AND WITH IT THE shining feeling, and the magic of it all was stuffed in the trash can, and January settled down to being winter with the first heavy snowfall of the season.

Stephie settled down, too, so deeply that she was hardly aware of being a junior and sloshing through March and sniffling well into April. Even the growing along with the going with Scott had steadied. Stephie guessed that looking the same and weighing the same and wearing the same sizes was a matter of finally being grown up. Not that she objected. She was fairly satisfied now with the way she had learned to cut her hair to hug her head like a brown seal cap, and wear colors that dramatized the green of her eyes, and be able to say five and a half B to the shoe salesmen without being measured.

But this business of being adult got rather dull at times in other ways, she decided. Oh, it was all right for people like parents who didn't mind being sort of picnic-companionable all of the time. But for herself and Scott, Stephie had to admit the easy familiarity they had drifted into got monotonous. Most of the time their togetherness took on a sort of old clothes feeling.

[69]

Take last night, for example. What was it he had said? Oh, yes. . . .

"I don't care. Whatever you want to do."

"Show?"

He started the car.

"Okay."

"Or just drive?"

"Sure." He tuned in a night ball game.

"Well, which?"

He sharply gestured her into silence as the sportscaster excitedly informed them that there the ball went . . . going, going, gone . . . foul. Scott swung the car out of town.

"What'd you say?"

Stephie slipped off her high heeled shoes and curled her feet up under her.

"Nothing. It doesn't make any difference."

"Why so distant?"

She sighed and put her head on his shoulder, tracing a finger down his shirt front.

"I know," he said. "I didn't bother to change. We weren't doing anything in particular."

"I didn't . . ." she began.

He laughed. "You didn't have to."

"We sound just like my parents."

"How?"

"Oh, knowing what we're going to say before we say it . . . among other things."

"Nice, huh?" He gave her a quick little squeeze. "Turn up the volume a little, will you?"

Stephie did, thinking as she did so of last December and her discovery that this something she and Scott shared had become sensible rather than just a wild thing of the senses. Now, she tried again to remind herself that though the old exhilaration was gone, so was the old depression and the no-middle feeling. And simply because the exhilaration was gone didn't mean that love was, too. It really was much saner this way, she reassured herself. And yet. . . .

Take this morning, for instance. He had whistled his arrival as usual and walked in without knocking.

"Ready?"

She gulped her milk, but was careful not to spill any on her new blouse, which had made even her father stop hunting his favorite cuff links long enough to comment on how pretty she looked.

"Just about."

His glance slipped off her as he helped himself to a hot baking powder biscuit.

"Um. . . ."

"Have another," her mother said, coming in from the kitchen. "You've plenty of time."

"No, thanks. Want to get there a bit early and arrange for a room for a committee meeting."

He got up and gracefully slid an arm around her waist.

"Remind me to eat here more often or else have my mother get your recipe."

Stephie watched her mother flush with pleasure and push him away with mock severity.

"Maybe you'd better go now," she said laughingly. "I'm not used to compliments so early in the morning."

Scott snapped his fingers at Stephie, jerking his head toward her mother.

"On your feet, girl. Orders from headquarters."

Stephie did as she was told, but not hurriedly. And as she collected her books from the hall table, she felt inexplicably discontented. Why, she didn't know. The day was spring and sunny. The general mood was happily intimate. Why should she resent the fact that he found baking powder biscuits more worthy of comment than a new peacock blue blouse? She shrugged and decided to attribute her lack of enthusiasm to the hot cereal her mother still insisted she eat every morning.

Tom Rodgers strode into the dining room with his usual cheerful morning male look and smelling aftershavish. "Stephie left yet?" he asked, sitting down to eggs, bacon, and biscuits.

"Just."

"Meant to tell her I was driving in and could give her a lift."

Edith Rodgers sat down to pour the coffee, chin in hand.

"Scott had to see about a room for some committee meeting or other, so they went early."

"My gray suit needs a button, by the way." He reached for the jam. "Why so glum?"

"You must mean the blue. I sewed one on the gray yesterday," she informed him, trying unsuccessfully to stifle a yawn.

"Poor Edith," he said with a sympathetic grin. "Stuck with a husband and child who are always rising and shining up to Mama for something. What did Stephie badger you for today?"

She poured herself another cup of coffee. "She wasn't

particularly shining this morning. She doesn't know it yet, but I think she's bored."

He had started to get up and sat down again.

"With what, for heaven's sake?"

"Scott. Going steady."

"How do you know? Did she. . . ."

"No. It's just apparent, that's all. In little things. There's a . . . a Sunday stillness about her . . . All dressed up and no place to go. There's a sameness about her, gestures, speech, expression, as though she had resigned herself to life being dull."

He got up and came around the table to give her his usual morning kiss which always came after his second cup of coffee.

"Happy?" he asked, nuzzling her cheek.

She sighed. "Yes. It's just . . . Well, I know you told me it would happen this way if I waited long enough, but I became so accustomed to the routine of waiting that I'd forgotten I was waiting. Now I'll have to go through it all over again with someone else."

"Well, I for one am kind of sorry. He's a likeable kid."

"Yes. I've grown rather fond of him in his own brash way."

"He's a little too cocky, but I suppose the army, when it gets to him, will knock that out of him in a hurry."

She smiled over a pile of dishes which she carried to the pass-through.

"That's just because he can play chess with you and talk to Stephie at the same time. And beat you."

His grin was more chagrin than anything else.

"Well, if it's true, I hope he can take it. He strikes me

as being a type that doesn't lose well. Hey, look at the time!"

Edith Rodgers would have been surprised had she known that not only did Stephie know it, but worried about it. It wasn't an every-minute-type of worry, she thought, coming out of school that afternoon. Mostly it came when she had nothing to do or think about.

She really didn't know why she worried at all. After all, it was only four months or so ago that she had thought it would be wonderful if Scott, also, could discover this . . . this grown-up . . . serenity? So why worry now when he had done just that? Settled down nicely into the routine of confining his telephone conversations to essentials, into sitting on the main floor instead of the balcony, into regarding kissing not as a breathless finale to a date, but as a gentle thing, an every day thing. This was really going steady. It was, she guessed, just that it got kind of dull at times. Like now.

Now was walking to Bronson's and sitting in the booth and waiting for Scott to join her after debate practice. Now was listening to the laughter from the other booths and seeing the boys lounging with Cokes and girls. Now was feeling April every time the door opened to admit another jostling, squealing group.

Stephie sniffed the air again as the door opened and closed once more. She returned purposefully to shredding straws, fighting down the inside restlessness.

"About two more straws worth ought to do it," Jim Stuart said, sliding into the seat opposite her. "He said to tell you he'll be along any minute."

Stephie didn't bother even to smile a greeting. Suddenly, everything seemed to come to a head . . . Scott and herself and the sameness . . . A spring that really wasn't Spring for her . . . and Jim. If it hadn't been for the attention he paid her last Christmas at that dance and Scott's jealousy and the scene that followed, she would still be giddy and . . . and girlish. Which, when you came right down to it, was more fun than this in-between feeling.

Stephie almost glared at Jim. There he sat, so content with everything and self-assured. Of late, he had, almost unnoticeably, become part of their crowd. Around and yet not around. Stephie wondered if he remembered that dance when he really spoke to her for the first time . . . the light, half-daring conversation with its exciting undercurrents that might have pulled them into something new had she been tempted rather than flattered.

Jim reached over and took the straws out of her hands.

"That's good practice if you want to turn into an old maid knitting afghans. Relax. Brooding doesn't help anything."

She snatched them back. Who was he to sit there so so . . . friendly and darn paternal?

"Don't pat me on the head!"

"I didn't."

"Oh, don't be so literal. You know what I mean." She pushed the straws away from her. "I'm not brooding and if I were it wouldn't be on account of Scott. I just don't happen to feel like being gay."

"How long has it been?"

"Has what been?"

"You and Scott . . . .

[75]

"A year," she answered quickly. "And three months and two days. Fooled you, didn't I?"

An angular smile cut into his face and he shook his head.

"No. No, you don't fool me."

She bristled. "You and your halfback strategy. Well, it won't work." She leaned forward with an intense look. "I'll give you something else to think about . . . I used to pretend. When I used to see John Wayne movies, Scott reminded me of John Wayne. Now when I see John Wayne movies, John Wayne reminds me of John Wayne."

He opened his mouth to interrupt but she stopped him.

"No, let me finish. All right, so before was silly . . . just dreams, and now I know what's real and what isn't. Simply because I'm tearing up straws doesn't mean I'm ready to fall into somebody else's arms."

He didn't say it offensively. "You're taking a lot for granted."

She was horrified at what she had said, but she couldn't stop herself and she went on as though she hadn't heard him. "Y'know, come to think of it, if John Wayne had to remind me of anybody it'd be you, strong, silent, un-smiling type that you are. Why don't you smile more, Jim?"

"I like to have a reason. I don't smile just to give my face something to do."

Stephie laughed and she had to work at it to keep the laugh from going wild. "Good old reasonable Jim. Everything has to be diagrammed for you, doesn't it? Well, don't break the pattern. You don't call the signals in a game, so don't try to make up for it off the field."

Something she couldn't name came into his face then, that frightened her and made her feel contrite at the same time. But before she could say anything, Scott dropped into the booth beside her.

"Better late, as they say, and you better agree," he grinned, casually putting an arm around her. Stephie was glad he did it in front of Jim. "What're we having?"

"Nothing for me. I was just going," Jim said.

Scott waved a friendly arm at him. "Don't go on account of me."

But Jim eased himself to his feet.

"I don't want to horn in on love's young . . ." He stopped.

"Dream," Stephie finished from within the circle of Scott's arm.

"No. No, that's not the word I want. Maybe you're right. Sometimes it's harder to face dreams than the real thing."

He nodded and walked away.

"Well, what're we having?" Scott asked again, withdrawing his arm.

Stephie looked at him wonderingly, and thought how typical it was of their new relationship that Scott didn't find Jim's remark cryptic. In fact, didn't resent Jim or anybody else who paid the slightest attention to her any more. Stephie told herself she was glad.

"Can the allowance stand a chocolate fudge sundae?"

"Nope. How about yours?"

Stephie dug out her wallet and handed him fifty cents. It had always given her satisfaction to share her allowance with Scott. There had always been something secure and intimate about it.

[77]

Scott's eyes moved over her face and his grin flashed again. "Better a Coke for you. Do I see the beginning of another chin?"

Stephie no longer minded his kidding, but she had to force the banter because of the mood she was in today. "The better to drool over you, my dear."

But the thought came that though she knew he was kidding, she also knew he was right in a way. Mentally, she was thinking fat and lazy. Most of the time. It wasn't like when they weren't going steady, when you kept thin in all ways, racing around hoping to see him, worrying about what she should wear in case she did see him.

Stephie stretched. "What are we doing tomorrow night?"

"Double date," Scott informed her, dumping fudge on his sundae.

"Barbara and Mac?"

"What's wrong with that?" he asked sharply. "I ran into him after History today. Maybe we'll go dancing.

"Well, you don't have to jump all over me. I merely asked who we were doubling with."

She stared at him, but saw nothing in his face to warrant the outburst. Maybe things hadn't gone right in debate practice. She didn't really care. All she cared about was the strange fact that she was almost glad to hear the sharpness in his voice. Anything, anything to relieve the dullness. And that, she thought with more bewilderment than distaste, is the craziest thing of all. When even a fight is preferable to the unruffled way things are now.

## ❧ Chapter ten

STEPHIE REALLY DIDN'T FIND THE REGULARITY OF THEIR double-dating peculiar. It was part of the cycle. As strangers, you started out double-dating, which became just the two of you as you got to know each other better, which reverted to double-dating when you got to know each other a whole lot better.

No, she didn't think their double-dating strange even when it more often than not meant Barbara and Mac. In fact she rather welcomed Barbara as part of the past when everything was good without reason and silly and uncomplicated, welcomed her red-headed vivacity.

Stephie caught a glimpse this Saturday of Barbara following Scott on the dance floor. Barbara always seemed as if she were barefoot even when she had shoes on. Stephie smiled and almost missed a step as Mac spun her around.

"I'm sorry," she laughed, guiltily. "Next time you're going to do that you'd better warn me."

Mac didn't smile. "I won't have to if you'll stop watching them," he said.

But Stephie wasn't looking at him or even listening to him. She was interrupted by another spin.

"I forgot the warning," Mac said, not sounding sorry at all. He looked a little sheepish. "I really didn't. It was the only way to get your attention." He paused and went on in a rush, "Look, don't you ever mind?"

Stephie at last looked up at him with surprise.

"Mind what?"

"Barbara. Scott. The way they kid around."

"They always kid around. It doesn't mean anything. Scott kids around with lots of girls."

"Well, don't you mind?"

"No. Once maybe. A long time ago. But even then I didn't really mind Barbara . . . Golly, I've grown up with Barbara, she's my Best Friend. She was . . . well, part of Scott and me from the very beginning."

"Take another look."

Stephie began to feel irritated.

"What's the matter, Mac, jealous?"

"Aren't Old Dog Trays supposed to be?"

Stephie shook her head. "You're an Old Dog Tray only if you think of yourself as one."

He swung her off the dance floor toward a nearby bench.

"Don't kid me, Steph. You know I take her out only if she's got nothing better on. Or else I'm just an excuse to be with you and Scott." He slumped on the bench. "It's harder, you know, to bring a new guy into the threesome. He might not want to go on double-dates all the time."

"Mac . . ." Stephie sat beside him, "You're all mixed-up . . . Look, I don't know who I am to be giving advice, but I do know this . . . I am a girl, and girls may think jealousy's fun at first but it sure gets tiresome after awhile and finally it's just plain hateful."

"I show what I feel," he mumbled, "and I can't help what I feel . . . I've got another date with her in three weeks but she'll think of something so we won't be alone. I told her we'd do something special. The two of us. But she'll think of something."

Barbara did.

"A party!" she cried, joining them, looking flushed and excited. "Let's have a party!"

Stephie glanced at Mac but he was looking almost apologetically at Barbara for having allowed his attention to be centered on Stephie so long. She turned back to Barbara and couldn't help smiling as she pirouetted round and round them and at last came to a stop again beside Scott, half leaning against him.

"For what?" Stephie asked.

Barbara pouted. "Oh, you're getting as bad as Mac. Do you have to have a reason for everything?"

"No."

"Well, then, let's have one! It's such fun planning a party!"

"When?"

Barbara put her arm through Scott's. "Well, Scott says he has to go to some old dinner with his father next Saturday, and I . . . well, I can't make it then, either, and the Saturday after that's the band concert, but the week after's all right." Her eyes dared Mac to contradict her. "How about you?"

Stephie looked at Mac and waited . . . but nothing happened. "It's all right with me," she finally said slowly, "but I thought you and Mac. . . ."

Mac didn't meet her eyes. "Well, I had sort of . . ." he began falteringly.

"Oh, that," Barbara interrupted. "We can do whatever we were going to do any old time." She flitted over to him. "Besides, you haven't actually planned anything yet, have you?"

"No. . . ."

She snuggled down on one end of the bench. Barbara never just sat.

"It's all settled then. Now, who'll we invite?"

Stephie edged over to make room for Scott, but he remained standing, jingling the coins in his pocket.

"First, where'll we invite them?" Stephie put in.

Barbara made a doleful face. "I can't have it. Mother's redecorating." She brightened. "What about your house, Stephie?"

"I don't know . . . Maybe. I can ask, anyway."

Stephie sat forward, feeling the sympathy for Mac wash out of her. Sure, Barbara stepped all over him, but it wasn't as bad as Mac's meekly surrendering to it. She was glad she didn't have Mac tied around her neck. No wonder Barbara kidded around . . . like with Scott, for instance.

"All right." Stephie leaned back again. "Who'll we invite?"

Barbara jumped up and began ticking names off on her fingers. "Let's see . . . Johnny and Jean, Ed and Lynn, Walt and Mary, Ken Williams and whoever he's going with at the time, and. . . ."

"Wait a minute! How many. . . ."

"Oh, let's make it a big party!" She glanced slyly at

[82]

Stephie. "You don't want to leave out Jim Stuart, do you?"

Stephie felt a little twitch of aggravation, but she had long ago learned to put up with Barbara's occasional innuendos because she knew that Barbara was like a child who might pull a dog's tail out of sheer mischievousness, but would never tie a can to it.

"Of course not," she replied firmly.

"He can bring that model, then," Barbara finished offhandedly. "That makes ten beside us."

"Model?" Stephie echoed.

"Why, yes. At least, that's what I heard, that he's dating some girl who's a model. I thought you knew."

Stephie wasn't going to let herself be trapped into a discussion, and, besides, she didn't really care.

"It's hard to keep track of all his girls," she said matter-of-factly.

Barbara smiled winningly. "Anyway," she flung out her arms and twirled around, "it'll be fun, won't it?"

Barbara's little-girl gaity couldn't be denied. Stephie had to smile back. "Yes. Yes, it will."

And it would, Stephie told herself an hour later after dropping Barbara and Mac off. She told Scott, too.

"It really will be fun."

He pulled into her driveway.

"We made good time. That new expressway really is a short cut."

"You certainly are subdued tonight. Don't you want to talk about the party?"

"Sure. Sure, it'll be fun."

"Barbara makes everything fun." Stephie yawned. "But sometimes she makes me feel old."

"Maybe that's the trouble." He frowned a little. "You. Me. We're not old, we're young. We don't have any fun anymore."

Stephie froze. They had it wrong, she thought. Ask a silly question and you get a serious answer.

"I didn't know you weren't having fun," she said icily. "You seemed content enough with the set-up."

"I didn't mean all the time. Just sometimes . . ." He fumbled the thought. "Oh, forget it."

"I won't forget it! You brought it up!"

And that, she thought, getting madder by the second, was the crux of the matter. He brought it up. Not herself, she who had been thinking along the same lines for a long time now. How could she have been so stupid to assume that only she was bored? Of course, in all fairness, he had given her no evidence of it, but then, neither had she given him any. And now she couldn't very well agree with him for fear it would seem like childish tit for tat.

He was silent.

She snapped open the car door.

"Well, when you think of some way to have fun, let me know."

She was half out of the car, slim leg outstretched, the moonlight creamy on one bare shoulder from which her stole had slipped.

He grabbed her other arm and pulled her back.

"You always were pretty when you were mad," he said, the words slurring a bit.

[84]

And, under his lips, Stephie remembered the thrill of making up. The bitter sweetness of it. Of resisting it and slowly succumbing to it.

Her fists slowly unclenched against his chest, and as her arms crept up around his neck, she thought, We haven't had to make up in a long time. Maybe this is what's wrong. Maybe we should make up more often.

## ⋙ Chapter eleven

IN THE WEEKS THAT FOLLOWED, GETTING READY FOR THE party, Stephie didn't have much time to wonder about Scott and herself. Her father had repainted the game room and her mother was preparing to do all sorts of wonderful and squishy things with whipped cream and little bottles of coloring.

However, she did know this much . . . she was glad Scott had brought it up, after all. Things were really much better between them. A new awareness, it was. Though she hadn't seen him with the usual frequency since it happened, the coming debate contest occupying him to the exclusion of everything else, each time she did a bit of the old feeling had been recaptured, a little of the old inside lurch. Best of all the lurch, because once she thought she had seen him driving by with Barbara, and though she knew she must be mistaken because he had practice that evening, she was glad of the twinge.

She had been standing with Jim Stuart on the steps of the public library when the car passed and Jim shifted his position, obstructing her view.

She moved around him and down the remaining steps.

"Lots of people have red Fords, Jim," she said, turning

and smiling back up at him. "But thanks, anyway. That was a nice thing to do, especially after the way I treated you that day in Bronson's."

She had the curious impression he was mad, and her smile faded as he joined her at the bottom.

"I really am sorry about Bronson's," she said, and instantly regretted referring to it again because she thought she must have been mistaken, for his face was as imperturbable as ever. She was even sorrier when he spoke.

"Don't be."

And the way he said it made it sound like nothing, but she had made it something and the least he could do was be gracious and let her, and why shouldn't she be sorry if she wanted to be?

"And I wasn't being nice," he informed her flatly. "I just happened to move at that time. But if you want to make something of it, that's up to you. Only don't drag me into it. Pretend by yourself."

She was right, he was mad. Not hopping mad or sulking mad. But quiet, controlled, impersonal mad that made everything he said sound more cutting and personal. She had to struggle to keep her voice as even as his own.

"But it wasn't Scott! He's at debate practice tonight."

"I didn't say it was. Was or wasn't, that's not the point. Why should I be nice about a thing like that?"

"Because anybody with any feeling at all for the other person would."

"I'm not anybody. That's the kind of hurt you should be hurt by, not protected from. Least of all by me."

"Why least of all?"

[87]

He considered for a moment and let it pass.

But Stephie didn't.

I'll tell you why," she threw at him. "Because you don't know what consideration is. You're so used to shoving people around on a football field, you play everybody off the field the same way. Rough."

He gave her a long hard look.

"If you want to think that, go ahead."

Stephie didn't and couldn't and she knew he knew it. No one was as gentle and understanding and easy to be with as Jim. It just seemed that recently all she did was get mad at him. Except tonight. He had started it tonight. She couldn't understand it. At least, with Scott, when he was mad you knew it, everybody knew it. And even when he wasn't, his conversation was to the point, a little dull and one-worded lately, but anyway he didn't just come close to talking about things. You never had to wonder what he was getting at. He didn't get at things. He got them out.

Her anger began to ebb and she merely sounded perplexed when she said, "I didn't think you didn't like Scott."

"I don't dislike him. It's envy."

"Envy? Of what?"

"You."

She looked startled and nearly grasped what they were really talking about when he smiled lightly at her and it slipped away.

"He's got you," he repeated in a teasing tone. "I wish I had a girl who, when my name was mentioned, jumped up as if it were *The Star-Spangled Banner*."

[88]

She had to smile.

"You mean your model doesn't? I know lots of girls who would."

"Model? Oh, Karen. I haven't been going with her long enough yet to find out."

"She's pretty, somebody said."

"More than that. Beautiful."

It was a statement of fact, she knew, but, for some reason or other, it bothered her. She shifted her books to the other arm, and in doing so caught her reflection in the polished body of a car parked at the curb, foreshortened, sweatery.

He reached out to take the books.

"I'll walk you home."

"Daddy's picking me up. Thanks, anyway."

She stood there feeling as much unlike a model as possible.

"Funny," she said at last. "I didn't know you were dating . . . Karen."

"That's because you're only interested in Scott. Nothing else really matters."

"I suppose so. If you want to keep something good, you've got to work at it and you don't have much time to think of anything else."

"Can't say I agree with you, but it agrees with you, so I guess it's all right."

"That's why I apologized about Bronson's before," she said insistently, a little appalled that she was back on it again, but feeling she had to make him accept her apology.

His face tightened.

[89]

"There you go again. I wish you'd stop being sorry, being polite. You're too darn polite. Even the nicest people aren't nice all the time. Sometimes you have to play rough. Then it wouldn't hurt so much when you run into someone or something that's not nice."

She began to feel uneasy and she wished her father would hurry up.

"I don't know what we're talking about, Jim," she said, worry creeping into her voice. "Are you trying to tell me something or is this your idea of small talk?"

He tossed off a quick smile.

"Sure," he assured her. "Sure. Small talk, that's all." He guided her toward her father's car, which had just pulled up. "Thought it would be more interesting than how are you, fine, how are you, I'm fine, too."

He refused a ride home and slammed the door on her, but not the subject, because the feeling persisted in Stephie that he wasn't sure, sure about it at all.

Stephie forgot about Jim's strange conversation during the remainder of the week. She was too busy trying to pick up her dress at the cleaner's on Wednesday and Aunt Margaret's chafing dish on Thursday and remind Barbara to be sure and bring her new Sinatra album. She felt too good about herself and Scott, her feeling of well-being, to remember anything she absolutely didn't have to.

That's why she didn't think of it again until Friday, the day before the party, when Scott picked her up in the car as she was walking home from school and forced her to recall it.

"Um . . . nice," Stephie said, sinking into the seat. "I'm referring to riding as opposed to walking, of course."

The car jerked as Scott shifted roughly into second. He scowled. "What else?"

"Well, I could have meant you, you know," she kidded him. "You might think I like you or something." She smiled softly. "Seriously, though, this is a nice surprise, seeing you. I didn't think anything could drag you away from debate practice."

"From what . . . oh, debate practice." He didn't look at her. "It's been keeping me pretty busy."

"Well, it won't last much longer."

She rested her head on the back of the seat. The sun beat in through the windshield, warming the good, good feeling inside her until she felt it would burst right out all over her like a rash. One block, two blocks went by.

Then, "I love to watch your hands on the wheel," she said languidly. "They're one of the nicest things about you."

"Don't say that." Sharply.

She raised her head. "Say what?"

"That. Nice things. Let the guys say them. A girl leaves herself wide open."

Stephie sat all the way up.

"I won't argue," she told herself as much as him in a small voice. "You're tired and all wound up with this debate thing. Maybe the party tomorrow night will help you relax."

They had pulled up in front of her house and she started to get out of the car.

"Don't go," he said swiftly. "Not yet."

[91]

She swung around happily and sort of melted back in beside him.

"Don't look like that," he begged.

Stephie's mouth said "What?" and stayed that way.

"I . . . There's something I have to tell you."

She groaned. "You don't mean you can't come to the party? That something. . . ."

"It's . . ." He stopped and looked away. "Do me a favor, will you? Turn your back to me. I can't tell you while you're looking at me."

"But. . . ."

"*Please*, Stephie."

She turned and looked out her side window. She saw all the familiar things . . . the house, and garden, and the two old oak trees that always looked as if they were bent double with laughter, and her parakeet sitting in the window . . . while she heard Scott say, "My folks think we're getting too serious. They want me to stop seeing you." She closed her eyes and looked again but everything was the same, except maybe the oak trees. Maybe she'd been wrong about the oak trees all along.

"That's . . . that's crazy!"

And even crazier was having Jim pop into her mind now of all times. Maybe she'd been right about feeling he wanted to tell her something the other night. But that was silly . . . he couldn't have known. Scott was just telling her this minute, now, Friday. It was coincidence with Jim, that's all. Like looking up a new word in the dictionary and then running across it again and again for weeks afterwards.

She half turned. "That's crazy!" she repeated.

"Don't turn around."

She stayed that way anyway, and found him looking miserable enough.

"But you know it's silly," Stephie insisted, really frightened now, her voice rising. "It's not as if we're going to run away and get married. Your mother and dad always liked me . . . Why they treated me like . . . maybe if we talk to them, tell them. . . ."

"No!" He said it almost too quickly. "I mean," he continued reasonably, "I've tried. It won't do any good. Not now, anyhow. You know parents. Next week it's something else. So if we let it sit for a while, they'll forget all about it."

"The party," she got out. "Everyone's invited, and what will I tell my mother? She's planned. . . ."

"Tell her nothing," Scott put in hastily. "I'll come to the party. But it will have to be our last date for a while until this all blows over."

"But . . ." she shook her head uncomprehendingly.

"Don't say anything to anybody," he pleaded, his eyes little-boy round. "Let's keep it a secret between us. Summer's coming up, anyway, and we won't see the crowd the way we do during the year. So we both date once in a while and someone in the bunch sees us with someone else. So what? It'll just look as though we've had a fight and by the time anyone else notices, we'll have eased back together again."

She turned all the way this time and he didn't try to stop her.

"How long?" she whispered, tears blurring her eyes and words.

"Please don't cry." He shoved his handkerchief at her. "I don't like it any better than you do."

"I'm sorry," she managed, crying anyway, remembering Jim's words the instant she said it, wondering if this was a time to be polite and decided it was because it really wasn't Scott's fault, it was his parents'.

"I don't know how long," he said, reaching over for her, moving his lips over her cheeks, the wetness of her lashes. "But don't be mad at Mother and Dad. It's not that they don't like you. They really do. They'll come around. It's just they've got a bug at the moment worrying whether we'll. . . ."

She scrubbed her face with the handkerchief. "I don't want to talk about it any more. It makes it real," she said, hiccuping the words. "I don't know how I'm going to get through the party tomorrow night."

"You'll get through it all right," he said softly, rubbing the back of her neck. "No more tears. It's not the end. C'mon now, give me a great big smile so I'll know you're not mad at me."

She tried very hard, clutching his handkerchief, and the smile trembled only slightly on her mouth.

"That's my girl. I couldn't stand going through this if I thought you were mad, if I thought I wouldn't be around in your thoughts in the meantime."

"Oh, Scott. . . ."

He held her tightly.

"And don't worry about the party," he told her. "Nobody will know."

## ✑§ Chapter twelve

BUT SCOTT WAS WRONG. EVERYONE DID KNOW. THAT SORT of thing gets around. The fact, not the details, but that was enough. How it got around so fast horrified her. No refuge was now possible in the numbness that had followed the muffled sobbing in a bathroom towel yesterday afternoon. Now, at the party, she had to be alive and bright and scintillating. She had to smile down the sympathetic glances, initiate conversation when there was an embarrassing lull.

Nobody was himself. Tense, strained, they all acted like strangers. Like Barbara who was oddly quiet outwardly. But every once in a while she gave Stephie the fleeting impression that she was having an awful lot of fun.

Time passed slowly. Too slowly for Stephie with her certainty that Scott would stay on after the others had left and assure her again that parents were crazy, that everything would be all right if they sat tight for a while.

Only Jim Stuart was his normal impersonal self. When Scott carried his buffet tray over to the staircase where Barbara was sitting, Jim drew Stephie down beside himself and his model.

[95]

Jim didn't make conversation. He commented on small things, and Stephie didn't have to think, or answer, or smile, or even nod. She was grateful for the respite that eased the strain and allowed her to gather herself together again for the leave-takings, of what a wonderful, wonderful party the horrible, horrible party had been.

She was at the door calling good-by to Lynn and Ed when Scott came up carrying his coat.

"It was a swell party," he told her with a broad smile.

Stephie stared at his coat.

"You're not going?"

His eyes quickly searched the room behind her.

"Mac couldn't get the car tonight, so I offered to drop him and Barbara off."

Barbara joined them, Mac trailing her.

"Tell Mac," she pouted prettily, "how perfectly silly it is for him to ride all the way home with us when it's really much better to drop him off first. Why, he'll be home in five minutes and the other way he'll have to wait simply hours for a bus back at this time and in all this rain."

"Rain?" Stephie echoed dully, hearing a clap of thunder and noticing for the first time raindrops beginning to darken the sidewalk.

Barbara tugged at Scott's hand, pulling him out. "Hurry! It's really starting to come down!"

Stephie didn't care. She had to say it. "But you're coming back?"

Scott half turned before ducking his head and starting to run toward the car.

"I don't think I'd better," he yelled over the thunder. "It's late and. . . ."

[96]

The rest of his words were lost in the rain and running footsteps.

Stephie wanted to run after him and cry out the wildness of the why, why, inside her, but instead she murmured, yes, yes, of course, very politely to the emptiness in front of her, and stepped backward into Jim Stuart.

She swayed a little and Jim steadied her. His grip tightened on her arms, squeezed out some of the blankness as he turned her toward his model who had one of those count to three smiles on her face.

"Oh," Stephie said, dragging one of her own up from somewhere. "I thought you'd gone."

"It was a lovely party," the girl said through her smile. "I'm glad you came."

"You won't be," Jim said, "if we stand here much longer. You're getting wet."

He stepped out, taking the girl with him, and Stephie closed the door, crumpling against it. She could hear her parents moving about upstairs and she pressed the back of her hand to her mouth to keep everything inside until she could make it up to her own room. If only they wouldn't stop her to ask how everything had gone. They'd have to know some time, but not now, not now.

She didn't know how long she slumped there. She felt rather than heard the light tapping suddenly from the other side of the door. He had come back, after all!

She clawed at the knob and flung the door open, every bit of her crying out her welcome.

"I can't find my car keys," Jim Stuart said. "I looked all over outside, but I must have dropped them in here."

And, feeling herself indeed coming apart, Stephie quickly turned and almost ran over to the far side of the

[97]

room, closing her eyes on the tears and her mouth on the ache in her throat, fumbling in the litter on table tops, kneeling and feeling under chairs and floor cushions.

"They . . . they must . . . must be here somewhere," she finally gasped, rising, keeping her back to him, fighting the great upsurge of emotion the effort to talk had released.

"Here they are," Jim announced. "They were in my suit pocket."

And Stephie, instantly realizing that he had known they were there all the time, wanted to cry out, don't be nice, Jim, not now, anyway, but couldn't because the tears had begun to slip slowly out, out.

He came up behind her and drew her back against him, letting her lean there, not trying to turn her around.

Stephie lay there passively, hands limp, the tears, unchecked now, streaming down her cheeks.

They stood there, unmoving for some time, and at last she straightened a little. He bent and kissed her lightly on top of the head, so lightly that she couldn't have been sure he had done it if he hadn't spoken.

"Good girl," he said softly. Adding, "It's not quite the same as a pat on the head. Remember that when you're remembering . . . other things."

He dropped his hands, then, and walked to the door. Stephie, still standing as he left her, heard it close quietly. And she thought, remember . . . Yes, that's it, remember . . . Remember that Scott had already told her that everything would work out if they just sat tight . . . What need for him to come back tonight and repeat it? Everything had already been said, so why go through even a temporary parting all over again? The sensible thing to do was to let the waiting period start and get it over with, she told herself.

She dried her face with her hands. She moved slowly, then, around the room turning off lights and started upstairs to her room.

Remember, Jim had said. It was silly to tell her that when that's all she would do, could do, in a sensible way, of course. And as for remembering Jim's . . . well, kiss of sorts . . . she didn't know how much room she had left to remember, though she had to admit she was rather tired of being sensible and that it might be kind of nice to squeeze it in somewhere, wonderful, friendly, just-right gesture that it was.

## ~§ Chapter thirteen

FUNNY HOW EVERYTHING SEEMED TO END AT ONCE—SCOTT
and spring and the school year. Stephie was painfully
aware of all three endings. Scott mostly. But the end of
spring saddened her, too, the end of the peeping time
when every day was a delight of discovery, a bit of green
protruding from a dull brown branch, a hint of violet in
the underbrush. Now there was nothing but for the days
to grow shorter, for all the growing things to stop and
stand still in all their oppressive fullness, with nothing
to do but finally fall or droop or disintegrate. Now was
summertime, with nothing to do since school was out
and Barbara's place at the lake was closed for remodeling.

Summertime was just what the song said it was, a
hush, baby, don't you cry time. This summertime, anyway. For Stephie. It seemed as if she had been living in
this state of hush forever, longer at least than the six
weeks it actually had been since the breakup with Scott.

And she didn't cry, either, except at first when it was
harder, just a little harder, to control her feelings. She
knew she had to tell her mother because Scott's absence
was bound to become noticeable and she was sure to ask
questions. Like. . . .

"You should get Scott to take you to that Alec

Guinness movie at the Starlight. You two haven't seen it yet, have you?"

"No."

Or was she likely to unless she went by herself, which she would never do, and if she did, she certainly wouldn't pick something funny, feeling the way she did. The last thing she wanted to do was laugh. Nothing was worse than having to laugh. It was betrayal, really.

Or,

"Did you give Scott that handkerchief he left here? I washed and ironed it and put it on your dresser."

"Um . . ." she murmered, hoping it would do as an answer, hating to be reminded of that day he had thrust it at her to wipe away the tear or two that immediately became three or four and more and more as soon as he said don't cry, please don't cry. She had examined the handkerchief carefully, and there wasn't anything on it but the "S" in one corner, but she was sure the tears were still there, unsoaped, unbleached, unpressed. She had hidden it underneath the horseshoes in her underwear drawer.

Or,

"We're having dinner with a business acquaintance of your father's," her mother told her one Saturday morning during the first hurting weeks. "Will you remember to be sure and close the windows before you and Scott leave? They're forecasting rain."

"Oh," Stephie said, and it sounded as though something was going to follow it but didn't.

Edith Rodgers, at the desk, looked up from her shopping list.

[101]

"No date?"

Stephie, prowling around the room, stopped before the big window, keeping her back to her mother.

"No date."

"Why . . ." Edith Rodgers started to say, and then she got it . . . it had happened! She looked down and added qrt. choc. chp. ice crm., Stephie's favorite, to her list. "Scott busy again?" she asked instead, wanting it confirmed.

"Yes . . . no . . ." Her voice began to quaver and she turned around then. "Oh, Mother," she wailed, "I'm so miserable!" And, seeing nothing but tears, she half stumbled across the room to her.

Edith Rodgers received the head in her lap and accepted the arms clutching her knees with the same old practiced comforting deftness that carried her back to Stephie's baby years.

She stroked her hair, the sobs somewhat subsiding under her hand.

"I know how you feel," she said softly. "Once I liked a boy and then I didn't like him any more, I just outgrew him, I guess, and I finally had to tell him that I couldn't ever like him that way again, and I felt miserable for days afterwards."

She stopped stroking as Stephie raised her head, the tears standing still in her eyes.

"But it turned out all right," she added, taking a handkerchief from her pocket and handing it to her. "He found someone else, in fact, four or five other girls before he married the last one who was much more suitable for him, and we became good friends."

"What are you talking about?"

"Why about this boy I used to...."

"I know that. I mean why are you telling me?"

Edith Rodgers was patient.

"To illustrate a point. The world hasn't come to an end simply because you've decided to break up with Scott."

"I decided? I didn't decide anything. His parents did."

It was her mother's turn to say it.

"What are you talking about?"

"If I decided anything it would be to go on forever and ever," she said, her voice beginning to break again. "But his mother and father thought we were getting too serious."

"Too serious," her mother echoed. Then, "Too serious?" as though she had just heard her. "If we didn't think it was too serious, why should they? I think I'll call Helen Parker and...."

Stephie was horrified. "No, Mother! No!" Almost hating his parents but not wanting her mother to hate them for fear the hate would carry over to Scott. "That would ruin everything!"

"If they don't want him to see you any more, what's there to ruin?"

Stephie rose to her feet, the bond broken.

Go to your parents when you're in trouble, all the articles on the women's pages always said. They're more understanding than you give them credit for. Ha! Come to your parents for understanding and what do you get? Logic. Plain old hateful logic.

"They're his parents," she said. "Scott feels as bad

about it as I do. I know I'd hate to have somebody call you up."

She looked kind of desperately at her mother and knew she wasn't reaching her.

"Why?" she almost screamed it at her. "Why did it have to happen?" The accusation in the why . . . all the things she wanted to say and couldn't, all the things she wanted to say and wouldn't, the accusation in her voice ". . . You're a mother, you're supposed to know."

Edith Rodgers flushed.

"Stop it, Stephie!" she commanded. "I won't have you carrying on this way!"

The tears froze in Stephie's eyes and her mouth closed over the sharp intake of breath.

"Anyway," her mother continued, "I never did approve of your going steady. You're much too young."

"But it's not what you make it sound like," Stephie ventured cautiously, stiff-lipped. "It's not serious, grown-up serious. You like someone better than anybody else and he likes you and so you go steady. Everyone does it."

Her mother dismissed the argument. "You're not everyone. You can't judge other boys or the men you'll meet later by one boy, one experience. You're not to see him again, Stephie. Do you understand?"

Stephie knew better than to risk another but. She was intuitive enough not to mention Scott's proposal that they wait out his parents' disapproval until it blew over. She permitted herself a wry little smile, but not until her mother's back was turned. Scott, she thought, hadn't counted on this, her own parents' reaction. She sighed. Another problem. But she was certain she could bring her mother around, and, if not, Scott could, when he started dating her again, with his quick smile and little-boy winsomeness.

So she had told her mother. She didn't make that mistake again.

"I wish we didn't have to go," Edith Rodgers said as they started to back out of the driveway.

Tom Rodgers looked in the rear-view mirror and saw himself. He jammed on the brakes.

"Why?" he asked, sounding annoyed as he adjusted it. "You'll like Ed and his wife. Besides, it's good business."

"I didn't mean them. I meant Stephie. She looked so forlorn."

He stopped once more and gave the mirror another tug. "What's she forlorn about?"

"It's happened," she told him. "Scott and herself. Finished."

"I thought you said she was ready for it. So she broke it off at last, so what?"

"He beat her to it. Or rather his parents did. Thought they were getting too serious."

"I don't believe it!"

She turned and looked at him. "Neither do I. And it's more than just instinct. I ran into Helen Parker at the supermart this afternoon."

"Did you ask her?"

"Heavens no! I couldn't embarrass Stephie."

He let out a sigh of relief. "What did you say to her?"

"Nothing, really. Just hello and will I see you at the Women's Club meeting next Tuesday and don't you hate to shop on Saturday and I guess we're blocking the aisle and good-by."

"Then why is it more than instinct? That conversation certainly doesn't indicate. . . ."

"Because she couldn't have been so natural. Her smile and manner couldn't have been so . . . so warm and . . . and real."

He shook his head, marveling at the female ability to feel an attitude and a head of cabbage at the same time.

"Well, if they didn't lay the law down, what's the explanation?"

"Much as I hate to face it, I'll have to. It seems that Scott broke it off before Stephie got up the courage to. He must have been as bored as she. And he just couldn't tell her the truth."

"Oh, Lord . . ." Supplication in the pronouncement.

"I know . . . She'll find somebody else, of course. But that's why I'm worried. If she should discover this before she does find somebody else . . ." Edith Rodgers let the thought hang there.

"You think Scott's found somebody else?"

"Probably."

"What can we do?"

"Nothing. Except hope the next one comes along fast."

He checked his watch with the dashboard clock. It was a nervous gesture because the dashboard clock always said six twenty-three.

"Look, Edith . . . Maybe we could have a quick dinner and make some excuse or other to get away early. You can call Stephie and tell her we'll be home to take her to a movie."

[106]

She looked at him with fond exasperation.

"That's sweet of you, Tom, but it wouldn't work. She'd rather be dead than seen at a movie with her parents on a Saturday night."

"Oh."

"I wish we weren't going out tonight, but maybe it's just as well. You have to do a certain amount of growing up alone."

Being alone wasn't for growing-up. Being alone was for pastel colored dreams about trailing down staircases to find Scott waiting for her at the bottom. Being alone was for writing in your diary about the exciting things he said to you that Tuesday you wore the new blue sweater.

Being alone was for listening to the sweet sad sounds of Sinatra when you could enjoy the aching sorrow you felt for other young lovers less fortunate than you.

Being alone certainly wasn't for listening to Sinatra when you became one of those others, agonizing over speculations on whom he was dating . . . someone utterly beautiful she knew or someone utterly beautiful she didn't know. She didn't know which was worse. All she did know was that she was sure to be beautiful. Utterly.

Being alone wasn't for trailing down stairs, even in dreams, now, because you knew all you'd find at the bottom would be the hall rug, one corner upturned where it was too high to fit under the front door when it was opened.

Stephie kicked it flat as she went by on her way to the kitchen and out the back door.

She sighed again and wondered how on earth she ever could have been bored with Scott. Bored with going steady and being sensible about the dullness of the familiar. The excitement of going steady and the fun, yes, even of being taken for granted had somehow dissipated into nothing. She didn't know how it got that way. Just one day the little breathless things were gone, holding hands, walking into the same room.

She shook her head. Well, she certainly wasn't bored now. The mere mention of his name was enough to start things thumping in her. There was more, she guessed, to this going steady than she thought. Maybe they used up too much emotion too soon. It was just, she decided, as she had told Jim that night in front of the library, that you've got to work at the little things so that they stay good.

She cut across the vacant lot next door and through the Cooper's back yard to Barbara's street.

Barbara had just finished taking a bath and Stephie wished she were putting on four petticoats and sandal-foot nylons instead of sitting in old denim shorts and watching.

"No date?" Barbara asked through her teeth as she opened a bobby pin with them and slipped it into her hair.

"No." She got out a little smile. "Thought I'd come over here and see how it feels to have one."

"Now I know you're kidding me! You went out with Jim Stuart only last week."

"He stopped by and we went for a drive. That's no date. It's like going out with my brother if I had a brother."

Barbara hooted. "Wouldn't I like to go out with a brother like that even if he was a brother!"

Stephie could feel herself flushing and was annoyed with herself because she didn't know why she should.

"Oh, you know what I mean."

Barbara looked at her curiously.

"You mean he's never tried to kiss you or anything?"

The flush deepened. "No. We're just friends. We talk. We talk about . . . things. All . . . all sorts of things. I can talk to Jim about . . . almost anything. It's sort of nice," she finished lamely.

"But not nice enough. If I had that . . ." she rolled her eyes expressively, "that boy around me I wouldn't waste my time talking."

"Barbara!"

"Oh, don't looked so shocked. You know as well as I do that almost any girl I could name would give her eye teeth to go out with Jim Stuart."

"Except me." Her face got a stubborn look. "It's not like that with us."

"Why? What are you waiting for?" Barbara's eyes narrowed. "For something to start all over again?"

Stephie bent down suddenly to tie a shoe lace that was already firmly tied.

"No," she said, hoping she didn't sound too startled and thinking Barbara always was good at shots in the dark. If she could only confide in someone . . . tell Barbara the truth about the break-up instead of having to keep silent about it, be evasive. But she knew that was impossible. For if it ever got back to Scott's parents that they were merely waiting them out, well, maybe they'd never change their minds.

"No," she said again, straightening up.

"You never did tell me why you and Scott broke up. I mean, the details."

"There weren't any details. We just decided to try playing the field for awhile."

Barbara had a funny look on her face.

"I mean what he said to you and you said to him."

"Honestly, I don't remember." Stephie met Barbara's eyes in the mirror, and it was Barbara who finally dropped hers and swung around.

"You should have let me know you didn't have a date," she said, getting up and going over to the closet. "Scott could have lined up somebody or other."

She ducked under the full skirt of a yellow cotton dress. "Zip me up, will you?"

"Scott?" Stephie echoed, repeating the name but not the offhand inflection.

"Yes, Scott. Some woman-type thing his mother belongs to is sponsoring this dance." She drew in her breath as Stephie tugged the zipper past her waist. "There's a hook and eye at the top. I knew you wouldn't care."

Stephie was glad Barbara's back was to her. Care? Of course, she cared! She was delighted! She fumbled happily with the hook and eye. Barbara! she thought. If she could have picked a girl for Scott to date in the meantime she couldn't have chosen anyone better than Barbara, her Best Friend. What a master stroke on Scott's part! He was really telling her she didn't have a thing to worry about. And she didn't. She didn't have to worry about Scott, and she certainly didn't have to worry about

Barbara who was too cute and fun and little-girl gay for any one boy.

Stephie couldn't resist smiling, but she did resist the desire to put her arms around Barbara's waist and hug her. Because Barbara would certainly know then that something funny was going on. And she wouldn't hurt her for the world by having her guess that Scott was using her as a stopgap until he could get back to herself.

Stephie shrugged. "Why should I mind?"

Barbara stared at her for a minute and then, in one of her rare bursts of affection, grabbed her hand.

"I know lots of nice people," she said, a strange note in her voice, "but you're so nice you make even the nice people seem not so nice."

*◈§ Chapter fourteen*

STEPHIE KNEW MOST OF THE NICE PEOPLE BARBARA DID
and Mac was one of the nicest of them all. Though his
lack of pride sometimes made her intolerant of him,
Stephie guessed that maybe love did that to you, and
was uncertain of her own strength if she were placed in
a similar situation with Scott. Not that she ever would
be. Stephie and Scott apart wasn't the same thing at all
as Barbara and Mac apart. For Barbara and Mac were
apart when they were together.

Stephie watched him pull over to the curb, his smile
leaning out the window with the rest of him. He certainly would be nice for some girl, she thought. Not
Barbara, but somebody who really liked him . . . always
ringing the bell and coming in, never honking his arrival,
always helping people in cars and across streets, always
giving people seats and benefits of doubts, too gentle to
argue, smiling, always smiling, whatever anybody wanted
to do being all right with him.

"How about coming down to the lake with me for a
swim?"

Stephie hesitated, shifting the bag of groceries from
one arm to the other.

"I don't know. I'd have to be back early. Jim's picking me up at seven."

"Oh, c'mon! I'll get you back. Hop in. I'll drive you home and you can pick up your suit."

She smiled. It was impossible not to smile with him.

"All right."

They got her suit and were down at the lake swimming out toward the raft in less than twenty minutes.

Stephie shivered as she pulled herself up on the raft.

Mac looked concerned as only he would ever think of being.

"Cold?"

She nodded. "Somehow you never expect the water to be cold when it's this warm."

"C'mon. I'll race you back."

He had already spread the blanket on the sand and was toweling himself when Stephie waded out.

"Want a Coke?"

"No, thanks. Not now, anyway." She began rubbing the sun tan oil on her arms and legs. "All I want to do is lie here and soak up the sun."

They stretched out on their backs, side by side, saying nothing, satisfied with silence.

Then, "Jim, huh?" Mac said, his eyes closed against the sun.

"Uh huh," she assented drowsily.

"You've been seeing him quite a lot lately. You like him?"

She opened her eyes as little as possible.

"That sounds more like a reproach than a question."

He rolled over on his side toward her, propping himself up on one elbow.

"I guess maybe I meant it to."

Her eyes flew wide open.

"You looked shocked," he said.

"I am."

"Why?"

"Because you're not the kind to say things like that. You never say things with double meanings. You always sound nice, say the nice thing, the . . . the. . . ."

"The dull thing. The ordinary thing."

"I didn't mean that and you know it." Though she knew she meant that, too, and knew he knew she did.

He flipped over on his stomach.

"Well, the worm has turned. I want an answer, so I'll ask it again. Do you like him?"

"Of course I like him! But not the way you think. It's just Jim, Mac. We've been friends for . . . for almost years. I'm not going to sit home. I'm going to play the field. Like Barbara. I don't have to like them to date them."

He didn't look at her, but she knew what she had done the instant the words were out.

It was too late, but she sat up, anyway, and put her hand on his arm.

"I'm sorry, Mac. I shouldn't have said that."

He shrugged, keeping his face pillowed on his arms.

"That's okay. It's true, let's face it. She'll never change . . . for me, anyway. But I wish you wouldn't act like that. You're not Barbara."

"It's just Jim, Mac," she said softly. "I can't pretend something that isn't there."

[114]

"Still Scott."

"Yes," wondering how much he knew, how much he guessed.

He sat up with an audible sigh of relief.

"I'm glad. Whenever I got real down over Barbara I always thought about you, and you made me remember that all girls aren't like her, that some really mean what they say and play it straight. And then I heard about you dating Jim so much, and I thought I was wrong, that they're all alike, because you got over Scott so easy."

"Easy?" she glared at him. "Do you call weeks and weeks of not seeing him, even once, even from a distance, easy?"

He dropped his eyes with obvious embarrassment. "Look, I know Scott gave you a raw deal," he said, tracing circles in the sand with a finger.

So he didn't know any more than the others, hadn't guessed how things really were. Stephie was sorry in a way that he hadn't because she could have shared the burden without actually breaking her promise to Scott.

"I didn't mean," he continued, "that I wanted you to hole up and die being true to him. All I meant was that I was glad you'd . . . what do they always say? . . . restored my faith in girls. I don't want to see you go through what I did . . . wanting, never getting. You've been a good friend to me. I wanted to return some of it. I'm going out and get myself another girl . . . quick. You should do the same. Maybe Jim's the answer, if you'll let him be."

Stephie evaded that. She smiled fondly at him and stretched out on her stomach.

"You have a watch? Give me twenty minutes on this side."

He dug it out of his pants pocket.

"I'm going to write Barbara off. Why should I keep bucking every Tom, Dick, Harry . . . and Scott?" he said meaningfully.

Stephie stirred uneasily. He was trying to warn her about Barbara and Scott. "Thank you for worrying about me, Mac," she told him with finality, "but don't. I'll be all right. You'll see," she added, trying not to sound as if she were full of secrets and thinking, I'll be all right, that is, if it doesn't go on much longer. If it does, I don't know what I'll do.

"Stephie. . . ."

She shut him off.

"I'll take that Coke now."

"Okay, okay. I can take a hint. The subject's closed."

He returned with Cokes and hot dogs and they spent the remainder of the afternoon sharing ideas and laughter and a bag of peanuts.

At the door, when he took her home, they stood for a moment, a little sad to be saying good-by, for they both sensed that it was really good-by.

"I hope you find her, Mac," she said softly.

"You, too," he echoed. "Give the guy a break, Stephie," he said wistfully, and with that, turned abruptly and ran to the car.

"Mac! Mac!"

He turned around briefly.

"I had such a nice time," she called.

And it was true. Everything was always nice with

[116]

Mac. She supposed it couldn't be any other way with one of the nicest people you'd ever want to meet.

Her mother finished straightening up the room.

"What time is Jim coming?"

"Seven, he said."

"Seven? Why, he'll be here in half an hour. Shouldn't you be getting ready?"

"I am ready."

"You're not going to wear that?"

*That* was a faded blue cotton she had changed into from her bathing suit.

Stephie got up wearily and started from the room.

"For heaven's sake, Stephie!" her mother called. "Jim's a nice boy. The least you can do is look your best."

Stephie didn't even turn around. She knew she could do something about the dress if she had to, but looking her best was a matter of feeling her best, and she couldn't very well go into her closet and take a feeling off a hanger no matter how nice a boy Jim was.

Nice. . . . She had to smile. Wouldn't the girls at school get a kick out of that? Cool, dreamy, smooth, maybe, but not nice. Not a big, sandy-haired, craggy-smiled football player. Even though he really was.

Stephie, thinking about what Mac had said, wondered why she couldn't get excited about Jim. Maybe because he acted as a sort of friend, around if you wanted to talk or even didn't want to talk, and either way it was comfortable, she had to admit, but certainly not exciting, his detachment. Which really kind of piqued her. Because Jim didn't know the break-up with Scott was only temporary. Yet he didn't move in. Or even try. Just around he was, not all around like Scott who was quick and volatile and demanded her every thought and emotion, creating them if necessary. She sometimes wondered why he dated her at all when they always acted like friends once removed.

She selected a dress at random from the closet.

He certainly was funny, she thought, dating her as though it didn't make any difference whether he dated her at all. Well, that went two ways. She didn't care, either.

She sighed. Things became so involved. Sometimes she thought it would be simpler if she did just sit home. The pretending was even harder than the waiting at times . . . pretending indifference to all things Scott.

## ☙ *Chapter fifteen*

FOR ONCE, STEPHIE REGRETTED JULY AND AUGUST BEING part of all the rest that have thirty-one. Before, she had always thought how wonderful it was that, of the almost two and a half months of vacation, two of those months should have extra days. Now all it meant was just that much more time to get through somehow. Jim made the somehow somewhat better than doing something alone. He took her mind, for a few hot hours at a time, off the hope which wouldn't stay as phlegmatic as the rest of her, that today, maybe today, Scott's parents would relent.

This August today was oppressive. Stephie was lying in the tub trying to soak away the heat when the phone rang. At that instant August could have been December. Heat, lassitude, everything that was this August fell away from her as she jumped out and threw a towel around herself. Hand on the receiver, she closed her eyes, praying let it be him, let it be him, and let it ring once more before shakily picking it up.

"Hello?"

"It's Jim."

She sank down on the couch. "I . . . I know."

"You sound funny."

"The heat must be bothering you, too," she replied, striving for lightness.

"No. And that's not what's bothering you. That's what I called about."

"It's too hot to play games. What?"

"Scott."

Stephie stiffened. It was the first time the name had been spoken between them since the party last May.

"What about him?" she asked, heart hammering, trying to sound indifferent.

"I thought maybe you'd heard. Some of the gang are going to that outdoor place on the lake to dance and asked us to go along. I accepted . . . before I knew Scott was going, too. So I thought I should check with you."

"Well, you've done it. What time are you picking me up?"

"Seven thirty. Then it's all right?"

"What difference does it make?" Her voice was a tonal shrug. "I'll be ready."

She hung up quickly, afraid to trust herself to further conversation. All right? It was wonderful! Wonderful seeing him for the first time since they had broken up. Maybe this was the way they could begin seeing each other again, at first in the same crowd, and little by little working up to the point where nobody would be surprised when they started dating once more.

Stephie rushed into her bedroom and yanked open the closet door. The pink would never do. Too insipid. She pushed hangers violently this way and that. Maybe the green, the far-away water kind of green.

She didn't hear her father come home. Probably because he didn't call out his customary greeting of, "Hello, the house!" and slam the door.

Tom Rodgers, his sleeves rolled up and carrying his coat, dragged wearily out to the kitchen where his wife was pouring tea over a pitcher of ice cubes.

"I'll have six glasses," he said.

She whirled around.

"Tom! You aren't sick? It's only a quarter of four."

He slumped in a chair.

"They let the office staff off early, so I decided to cut out, too. If this heat continues, they'll have to put in air conditioning." He took off his tie. "Where's Stephie?"

"In her room."

"Bad little girl been banished?"

"Bad? No." She squeezed the lemons with short, deft twists. "Good and stupid."

She poured the lemon juice in the pitcher and turned around. "Oh, Tom, I'm worried. I wish you'd talk to her. I've tried, but it doesn't do any good. Hearing the facts from you might have more effect." She turned back to the counter. "About Scott and Barbara, I mean."

"So that's it," he said reflectively. "I wish you'd let me know what's going on. I never would have known or believed it if I hadn't seen them today, parked in front of her house. They broke apart as I drove by."

Her shoulders sagged. "I thought I had told you about it. Some days I don't know what I'm doing, what with Stephie and this heat. I've seen them several times myself, together, and there's something about them that makes it seem more than just once in a while dating as Stephie says it is."

"Stephie says?"

She looked uncertain.

"I don't suppose it was the right thing to do, but I told her I had seen them. She's been acting so funny lately."

"You mean she still likes him?" he asked incredulously.

She nodded, "But it's more than that. I get the feeling that she's waiting for something, biding her time. My guess is that he told her they'd go back together again when his parents cooled off."

"Surely you told her it wasn't his parents after this length of time?"

"No." She poured the iced tea into frosted glasses and brought them over to the table.

"I couldn't tell her a thing like that unless she'd found somebody else. And Jim's not the answer. Not yet, anyway."

He got up and walked over and put his arm around his wife.

"Don't worry . . . Do I have time before dinner to have a talk with her?"

She turned in the circle of his arm.

"Oh, yes, Tom! If you only would. Maybe she'll listen to you."

He smiled somewhat grimly.

"She'll listen, all right. If I have to make like a teenager to talk some sense into her."

Tom Rodgers tapped lightly on the half-open door of Stephie's room and then poked his head in cautiously. Even more startling than not finding her moodily balled up in the slipper chair by the window was the lilt in her voice.

"Daddy! Come in!"

He stretched out his arms to catch the swooping figure who came to a ladylike stop a foot away from him and decorously offered her cheek for his kiss.

"You stopped just in time," he told her, brushing the kiss on. "I was afraid you expected me to toss you up in the air." He grinned ruefully. "I'm not as young as I used to be."

"Oh, I don't know . . . I still think you could do it." She started to back up, eyeing him impishly.

"No, you don't!" He reached out and grabbed her and then held her there at arms' length. "Hey! What's all this?"

"What's all what?"

He sniffed appreciatively while taking in the lace petticoat frothing below the hemline of her short robe, the dresses heaped on the bed, the jewelry strewn in sparkling confusion on the dresser.

"Perfume and dancing slippers," he said. "Big date?"

She wiggled out of his grasp.

"Nothing special. Just Jim."

"All this for just Jim?" he asked teasingly, thinking mothers were as crazy as kids sometimes, worrying over nothing.

Stephie put the green dress aside and vanished into the closet.

"We're going dancing with some of the crowd."

"I like Jim," he told her, trying to provoke her into some sort of an answer to just Jim. Though the answer was obvious . . . all the finery, the perfume, the high color in her cheeks.

"Most people do," she said from the depths of the closet.

[123]

Something in her voice, muffled or not, made him look up from the jewelry he was aimlessly poking among on the dresser.

"Don't you?"

She emerged from the closet looking a little touseled, holding a yellow dress.

"Sure."

She stood still for a moment, considering the dresses, while he tried to fold himself into the slipper chair and gave up.

"That's a nice dress," he said, indicating the sea green silk billow, while searching for a topic and a place to sit on the bed.

"I want to look nice," she told him. "I haven't seen some of the kids we're going with since school let out. Girls can be kind of catty if you don't look right."

Girls? he thought. Kids she hadn't seen since school let out. Suspicion began to gnaw at his thoughts. No girl dresses for another girl. She dresses for a boy. And if it wasn't Jim. . . .

"Scott going to be there?" he asked casually.

She sat down at the vanity table and began brushing her hair.

"Maybe."

"Maybe?"

Her head snapped upright and her eyes met his in the mirror.

"All right, he is! So what?" She bent her head and renewed the vigorous brushing.

He got up and walked over to her.

"Look, Stephie," he said, putting his hands on her

shoulders, "why eat your heart out? Face it. He's not for you."

Her shoulders remained rigid under his hands.

"You certainly thought he was once!"

"He was all right for a start. But you've got to go forward, not back." He awkwardly tried to pat her. "Look Stephie . . . You were just too young to keep it alive. You were together too much. There's nothing wrong with either of you that a little growing up won't fix."

"The only one there's anything wrong with is you!"

He felt the anger rising in him and didn't wait for it to subside.

"All right, since I can't talk to you as an adult, I'll have to treat you like a child. He's brash and shallow and too familiar."

"Go ahead and hate him. He doesn't care whether you like him or not!"

"Don't kid yourself. It's a basic urge. We all want the approval of others."

Her chin set stubbornly. "You don't understand."

He sighed and went back and sat down on the bed.

"I dislike him," he said slowly, thinking out loud, "because of what he has done to you. I have to admit he probably did what any male would under similar circumstances, lying his way out. I can understand that."

He looked at her for a minute and then forced himself to be pitiless.

"But I can't understand you," he said harshly. "Still eating your heart out over a boy who got rid of you for someone else. He must have handed you a whale of a story."

Her voice wavered a little. "There's nothing to it."

"He dates Barbara, doesn't he?"

"Yes. But you don't seem to get it. Barbara's my Best Friend."

"Why?" he pleaded almost desperately. "Barbara can't be a best friend even to herself. You ought to know that after all these years!"

Stephie could have told him why. Barbara was bright and daring and knowledgeable. She knew all the real fun places to play, though it was always Stephie who tore her dress climbing the lumber forms of a new house or got all snowsuit soggy because Barbara decided at the last moment that she couldn't even try to stop the sled at the bottom of the hill where the thinly iced brook ran. Barbara thought of the hardest clues for treasure hunts. She knew how to catch a butterfly and why a lightning bug lighted and what was the best sun tan oil and when to pass a note in school or a boy's house if the lawn needed mowing. What she didn't know, she sensed or guessed. And she always hit it exactly right.

Stephie could have told him. Told him that she never wanted someone like herself for a Best Friend. Someone shy and sensitive and unsure. You never got any answers that way. It would be like talking to yourself. But she didn't even try to tell him because she knew he wouldn't understand. So she sat there, staring hostilely at him.

Tom Rodgers got up wearily and walked to the door.

"You're right," he told her. "Every kid is right when he says his parents don't understand him. I don't understand you. I hope you understand yourself."

Closing the door behind him, he rubbed his hand over

his forehead. If I went in a teen-ager, he thought, I came out a father.

She was ready when Jim came. A long time ready. She was happy and vivacious and excited.

"Do you really want to go?" Jim asked again when he got the car started. "We can always go somewhere else."

"Oh, that's as good as anything," she murmured disinterestedly when she actually wanted to shout hurry, hurry!

"He'll have a date, you know."

"Of course he'll have a date! We agreed to. That's part of it!" and almost clapped her hand to her mouth.

The car slowed down suddenly as he turned to look at her.

"Part of it? Part of what?"

Stephie knew she was half-way committed now, but she skirted the subject warily.

"Well, when we broke up. We decided . . . things." Thinking it wouldn't hurt now to tell Jim the way things really were, to tell everybody. Because tonight was sure to be the start of starting over.

"Decided what?" he asked with irritating patience. "You broke up because . . ."

"Because his parents thought we were getting too serious."

He stared at her incredulously. "He told you that?"

Stephie returned the stare angrily. "That happens to be the way it is. We didn't break up because we wanted to!"

Jim pushed his foot down hard on the accelerator. "You're using 'we' rather loosely, aren't you?"

[127]

"Do you have to really work at being nasty or does it just come naturally?"

He slammed the car into a parking space behind the pier and cut the motor.

"Look, I'm just trying to tell you to prepare. . . ."

"Tell me what?" she demanded. "Tell me something you've dreamed up? No, I'll tell you. Scott and I are just marking time until it all blows over and then we'll ease back to where we left off!"

"He isn't going to ease back into anything! He was letting you down easy!"

She tugged at the handle, shoving the door open.

He grabbed her wrist. "Just a minute! Before you flounce out of here, suppose you tell me what I am . . . a fill-in?"

Stephie had never seen Jim really and truly angry before. The closest he had come to it was that night at the library and this wasn't anything like that. It was frightening because it was quiet, controlled, not pushing him around.

"Don't, Jim! You're hurting me!"

His fingers tightened.

"I'm waiting."

She stopped trying to pull away from him.

"I . . . I don't know what you are," she confessed falteringly. "You're a . . . friend . . . I guess. . . ."

His grip on her wrist relaxed. "What a dope I am," he muttered tiredly. "Thinking you were grown up when you were really just plain gullible."

"What do you mean, gullible?" she said, feeling the anger squishing through her again.

[128]

"Nothing." He clamped his mouth tight on the word.

"That's right, nothing. That's the first thing you've said so far that's right. I'm going in," she informed him.

He almost threw her arm at her. "Go on!" His voice roughened. "Go on in there, then, and see for yourself!"

And she did, Jim deliberately lagging behind. But running out on the pier to the pavillion, she stopped short, the waves, music, and voices lapping around her. She waited for him to catch up to her, suddenly unsure, not knowing just what she would find inside.

But she found only what she had expected. Barbara and Scott and the old crowd around a big table in a far corner.

Barbara waved merrily.

"What took you so long?" she called from the end of the long table. "Don't you two know parking comes after, not before?"

Stephie flushed, feeling a faint premonition. No answer was really required to Barbara's question, but the hanging implication made her kind of nervous nevertheless.

Stephie dared to look fully at Scott for the first time, the dark, thin intensity of him, and for once, the familiar seemed exciting. When his eyes finally met hers, she smiled tremulously, trying to reassure him.

"How've you been?" he asked brightly, hating, she was sure, the necessary banality as much as she.

It didn't require an answer, either, though she wanted to tell him right then, awful, perfectly awful. But that would come later when he asked her to dance, when they could talk alone.

The band started up again. Maybe now, when they'd

all get up to dance, and after a number or two he could properly stop next to herself and Jim on the floor and suggest changing partners.

If Jim would ask her to dance. If he'd only stop staring impassively out the window and ask her to dance. She got desperate, and then mad, and when he finally inquired coldly, "Do you want to dance?" she was up and half-way to the floor almost before the words were out.

He looked at her strangely, but didn't say anything, and she was glad because she couldn't talk and dance with Jim at the same time. Maybe because she was used to Scott's effortless style, the lightness, the twirling elation. Jim, because he was big and sort of all-enveloping, moved slowly and almost imperceptibly, with the rhythm of a heavy animal.

Stephie spotted Scott and Barbara almost immediately. Holding herself rigid, she tried to maneuver Jim toward them, but the four of them might as well have been dancing on different floors for all her efforts. She wanted to pound her fists against his chest and push him next to them, the frustration was so great. But two numbers later, when they were in almost exactly the same spot from which they had started, she gave up. And then, miraculously, when the next number ended, there they were right beside Scott and Barbara.

They made small talk for a minute. When the music started again, Stephie took a little expectant step away from Jim's side . . . only to be left standing there while Barbara possessively took Scott's hand and danced away.

"I'm over here," Jim said.

Stephie turned vaguely to him, limp now in his arms.
"That's better," he commented.
"Wh-what's better?"
"Me leading."
The shock and disappointment fell away.

You think you're so smart, she thought. Well, you'll see. Scott will ask me to dance. When we're back at the table. In front of everybody. That way is even better.

And when they got back to the table, she chatted animatedly with everyone. She didn't mind waiting. In fact, it was kind of fun waiting, knowing that when the orchestra began playing once more he would speak her name from his end of the table and ask her to dance. Or maybe he'd come up behind her and merely put his hand on her shoulder. Either way, she'd be talking gaily with Lynn on her right, certainly not Jim who had gone back to staring moodily out the window, and she'd raise her head and smile one of those smiles that don't need any words to go along with it.

When the music suddenly blared out, it blasted the conversation and Stephie both. One piece of her was politely listening to the talk, another to the music, and another for the sound of Scott's voice. As the music swung from introduction into melody, she became a little panicky. If Lynn would only stop talking! She'd never hear Scott even if he shouted. When Lynn leaned over to pick up her glass, Stephie quickly tried to run her eyes across and down the table to Scott, but she couldn't quite make it around her. She gave it up, reassuring herself that he'd probably walk over to ask her, anyway. She even began to get the smile ready. But she

[131]

had to give that up, too, when the table finally cleared out and only she and Jim were left sitting there.

More astonished than anything else, she watched Scott and Barbara melt into motion on the floor, ready to avert her eyes whenever he looked her way. But he never did.

She stopped being astonished several dance sets later as time after time the table emptied but for herself and Jim. Stricken, she wondered why, what had she done? Had she appeared too distant, too disinterested? Or had she seemed too eager, her eyes giving her away?

She reached the point where she didn't know where to look. She couldn't stare at the dance floor any longer, and she couldn't constantly be searching through the contents of her bag or running to the refuge of the powder room. Besides, she hated looking at herself almost as much as at Barbara, her cheek against Scott's, eyes closed, sort of curled up on his shoulder.

Smiling tentatively, she edged a little closer to Jim who was now making intricate designs with pretzel sticks.

"It won't do any good," he said, without raising his eyes. "He isn't looking this way."

She took it. She had to. "I know," she admitted in a small voice.

He lifted his head, then, and looked at her. "Do you want to go?" he asked more gently.

"No." She gestured gaily as Scott and Barbara twirled by their table. "Everyone's going to the Barn later for hamburgers."

Jim abruptly swept the pretzel sticks aside.

"Haven't you had enough?"

"No," she said again. "There has to be some reason,

some explanation. There has to be . . ." Knowing now, sick with the knowing for sure that everyone had been right about Barbara. But not Scott. Not Scott. . . .

So they followed the rest of them to the Barn, and they all went in and sat around another big table. All, that is, except Scott and Barbara whose places were left next to Stephie and Jim.

"Scott must be lost," someone said. "Did anyone give him directions?"

"The only lost he is, is in a dream," someone else sang in throbbing ballad tones.

But Stephie wasn't really listening. She was thinking with conviction, now, now, I'll know. When he comes in and sits down beside me. Surely he can't sit next to me and say nothing.

They waited for the waitress to take their orders.

They waited for Scott and Barbara.

They waited for the waitress to bring their orders.

They waited for Scott and Barbara.

The orders came. Stephie ate her hamburger slowly, very slowly, not looking at the empty seat next to her, telling herself that two bites from now it would be filled, one, two, empty still. Two more bites, then, trying to close her ears to the titterings about the parking area half a mile down the road, fighting the desire to scream out loud that they might have had an accident.

And then they came, hand in hand, smiling broadly, not even bothering to be self-conscious about the sly comments, the not-so-sly questions.

Stephie didn't need to see the smudge of lipstick he hadn't quite wiped off to know where he'd been.

She had half a hamburger to go yet, and she thought

[133]

dazedly, one thing at a time, I'll take one thing at a time.

Scott sat down beside her, rumpling her hair with easy familiarity.

"Sure haven't seen much of you tonight. What's new?"

And she could have told him, just the same old feeling, the same old feeling. Instead, she said, "Nothing."

Jim turned to her. "How about now?" he asked in a low voice. "Do you want to go now?"

She sat up a little straighter and shook her head. "I haven't quite finished yet."

And she went on with it, got through with it, passed the salt when Barbara pertly demanded it, leaned forward and passed adequate enough replies around Jim when Barbara addressed her. She even managed to be quite gay with the farewells when they all gathered outside.

One thing at a time, she told herself again when she was back in the car with Jim and on her way home. I'll think about it when I get home. But just the thinking of thinking about it later unleashed everything right then and it all crowded around in her until she couldn't separate one emotion from the other. She felt all crumpled up inside like a rayon dress pressed with a linen-hot iron.

"How could I have been so stupid?" she finally burst out.

Jim didn't make it any easier, but at least he didn't say I told you so.

"Maybe feeling the way you do about somebody makes it easy."

She clenched and unclenched her hands. "I hate him!"

"Do you?" he asked quietly.

"Yes! I'm mad! Clear-through mad!"

"And jealous?"

"No! Why should I be jealous?"

"Oh, jealousy has its uses. Like pepper. It can be used to bring a guy back into line. Sometimes it's better than pretending that you couldn't care less."

"I'm not pretending! I couldn't care less! The only thing I care about is all my so-called friends knowing and not coming right out and telling me."

"Feeling a little sorry for yourself?"

"That's natural under the circumstances, isn't it?"

He pulled up in front of her house and cut the motor. He turned toward her. "Look, I'm going to tell you a few things at the risk of seeming like a heel, but I don't know why everyone else should have to stay after school because Scott was a bad boy. So everyone's known all along that Scott was dating Barbara before you two broke up, but. . . ."

"As long ago as that?" Stephie breathed.

"No one was really surprised when the news hit the night before your party that you two were breaking up."

"But . . . but how. . . .?"

"Barbara saw to that. She dropped a word here and there that you were out and she was in."

"Barbara . . ." Stephie whispered. The tears started rolling slowly down her cheeks and he reached over and shook her slightly.

"Look," he said earnestly, "what I'm getting at is this . . . Sure, everyone knew, but they thought, as I did, that you had tumbled to Scott and really didn't care because you were kind of tired of the whole thing, anyway. Even when I found you crying that night I supposed you were just sad about the bad ending when everything . . . well, once had been good."

The tears began to come faster and his hands tightened on her shoulders.

"Don't you get it? They thought the brush-off was yours as much as his. That you went through with the party because it was too late to call it off. Nobody was laughing at you. Don't feel sorry for yourself, because nobody else does."

She crumpled against him, sobbing now, and he slid his arms around her and bent his head, her hair muffling his words.

"If I thought I could make you hate him," he said fiercely, "I'd call him everything I could think of. I'd even make up things if I thought that."

He drew back a little, forcing her head up.

"Before this, before tonight, I intended to try to move into Scott's place. But something about you bothered me. Your attitude about Scott. You didn't quite ring true. It's a good thing I didn't really try. That's right, isn't it? You don't really hate him even now, do you?"

She met his eyes and didn't waver.

"No," she said, "I guess you don't turn those things on and off."

He accepted it. "Thanks." And meant it.

"About the best thing I do is use you as a wailing wall, doing just what you said I'd do . . . falling apart." She smiled faintly. "But you know what? With all these horrible feelings filling me up, I ate that hamburger not because I had to but because I wanted to. I was hungry."

He laughed for the first time that night. "You'll live!"

She laughed with him, still in the circle of his arm, feeling the strength of it. Suddenly her laughter trailed off, and she looked at him, and she wondered wildly what

[136]

she was thinking of, telling him it was still Scott, and now feeling, feeling something, wishing something. . . .

And Jim, seeing the want in her eyes bent slowly over her. He stopped half-way and swung her roughly over to her side of the seat.

"Not this way," he said harshly. "Not on the rebound. When I kiss you, it's going to be good, not half-good. Kissing's a matter of give and take, too, you know."

Feeling the shame course through her, she sat in the same crumpled up position in which he had placed her.

"Some day you'll come to me," he went on, "and it's got to be that way, your coming to me, you understand that, don't you? You'll come to me and you'll say it's off with Scott, the way you feel about him, I mean, and you'll tell me it may not be on with me yet but you'd like to give it a try."

She nodded.

"Some day," he repeated. "It may not be tomorrow or a week from Tuesday, but it will happen. And we'll see how good it can be. It may not be, but we'll try it."

He opened the door and got out and walked around to her side, Stephie meanwhile wondering why it was that all the wrong people said the right things.

The night air was still hot and humid.

"Summer," Jim commented. "You'd never think fall was so close. Just think . . . Couple of weeks and we'll be seniors."

Stephie sniffed the air. Summertime, she thought wryly, when the livin' is easy . . . a hush, baby, don't you cry time. . . . Well, she was too tired to cry any more tonight. Crying was for later.

## ❧ *Chapter sixteen*

JUST THINK, JIM HAD SAID WITH A VOCAL EXCLAMATION
point, couple of weeks and we'll be seniors. Well, there
was nothing exclamatory about it at all. A senior. Funny
about being a senior. For some reason Stephie had always
thought it should be capitalized. But there really wasn't
anything capital S about it either. You learned to remember to write 4B instead of 3A after your name on homework assignments. You learned that Virgil wasn't any
easier than Cicero. You learned that Scott was going
steady with Barbara.

Stephie sighed and hated herself for doing so, but at
least she was sighing now instead of crying. Sighing and
hating herself because she still wanted Scott, nice, not so
nice, any old way at all. Time and shame and disillusion-
ment might have turned the tears into sighs, but she
didn't know what it might take to turn the sighs, not
into something else, but just off.

Anyway, there it was. There was little she could do
about it, though she did try, almost frantically, that first
month back at school. She tried with Ralph Cooper who
was sharp and strenuous and sports editor of the school
paper. She tried with Bob Willis who was self-effacing

and studious and was sure to graduate first in the class. She tried with Joe Shannon who was sweet and smooth and played a trumpet in the school dance band. But it didn't work. None of them interested her enough to dispel the image of Scott for more than a few minutes at a time. If they went to a movie, his laugh, coming too late or too soon, never quite blended with hers. If they went dancing, the arms holding her were either too loose or too tight and just not Scott's. So she did try. But not with Jim who might have helped. Never with Jim, because Jim had told her it couldn't be him until she was sure that Scott was stilled forever instead of being unsure about it still being Scott.

Stephie got a little panicky at times over the knowing of maybe never knowing. More depressed than anything else this late September day, she slid the tray along the cafeteria counter, soup, salad, milk, and dug in her purse for change.

"You should eat more than that if you're going to carry a big torch."

She swung around. "Oh, hi, Jim."

He tilted a smile back at her and waved an arm. "There's an empty table over here." He led the way in and around people and chairs.

As Stephie followed him, she felt eyes on them. She wondered if she turned suddenly what look she would surprise in the. . . . No, not surprise. She knew what she'd find . . . adoration, envy, conjecture . . . They always adored the big ones, the football players, especially ones like Jim with a sameness of coloring that made the bigness seem even bigger . . . always envied the girl with them . . . and the conjecture? Well, her guess was as good as theirs as to why she treated Jim like any old anybody. She didn't know why, because she was attracted to him.

She took the food off her tray and handed it to him, glad of distracting lunchroom noises. Ever since that horrible night when she had wanted him to kiss her, she felt embarrassed with him.

Since then, of course, she hadn't dated him, and maybe he was right, she wasn't ready for him yet. But it embarrassed her nevertheless to see him now and know she could respond to him and yet persist in her feelings for Scott.

Stephie toyed with her soup, waiting.

And then it came.

"Well, how's the torch?"

She put down her spoon and looked at him, suddenly going a little weak with that same melting something she had felt with him in the car that night.

"I'm tired of it all," she said in a little whisper. "Waiting for the time to come when I can look at him and not feel anything, even hate. Your some day hasn't come yet, but how can I get rid of old feelings if I don't get a chance to know any new ones?"

"You've been dating some pretty interesting guys. I'm sure they'd give you the chance if you looked at them the way you did at me in the car that night."

Her face drained of color as she stood up.

"I'm not that kind of . . ." she began, shock and hurt choking her voice.

"Sit down." It was an order, not a plea. "I know you're not that kind. I said it because I want to hear that it

[140]

wouldn't work with those guys for the simple reason that you like me, not them. Go on, say it! It'll be a real novelty. I've waited long enough to hear it."

She sat, heart pounding.

"All right . . ." She faced him like an elocution class and got it out fairly slow and clear. "Can we try it now, Jim, you and I? You're the only one who can make it work if it's ever going to work."

He leaned back. "I'm tempted," he said matter-of-factly. "I'm really tempted." He leaned forward again and reached for his bottle of milk. "But the answer is no."

She started.

"Because," he continued, "the only thing I'm interested in working on is us, you and me, not you and me and Scott." He was almost belligerent. "Why should I start out with one strike against me? I'd get to know you, really know you . . . whether you cry at movies, if you like onions on your hamburger, what makes you laugh . . . and where would that leave me? Right back where I started . . . with Scott's girl."

Stephie lowered her eyes and fumbled with her books.

"You seem pretty sure it would be . . . that way."

"I don't know that it would, but it could."

She gathered up her books somewhat impatiently.

"Well, of course. Anything could happen. A . . . A bomb could fall on us, or. . . ."

"Or Scott could come crawling back and say sorry I've been a bad boy but let's give it another go. That type always does, you know. They can't stand the same thing too long. Or if they see you're going with someone else and think you find the someone else more attractive

[141]

than they, that alone would make them come back." He paused. "Or has that idea already occurred to you?"

She didn't get mad. "No. Should it have?"

He almost grinned. "Okay, so that was another nasty crack. I'm sorry. But I'd still like to know what you do."

"I'd tell him. I'd tell him I liked somebody else."

"And if he came back before you had time to . . . to like somebody else?"

She was quite serious, but she smiled a little.

"I'd let you know, Jim, so you could get out in time."

"And if he came back later, when I was in so deep I might not want to get out and you still hadn't changed toward him, what then?"

"If . . . if I'm going with you, I . . . have a feeling that I won't be thinking about Scott any more." She blushed. "That's the closest thing to a sure thing I can think of."

He sat there looking, looking at her and finally she had to ask it.

"Well?"

The bell rang for the next class and she laughed somewhat shakily.

"Saved by the bell." She stood up. "I've got a one o'clock, so. . . ."

Nothing from Jim.

She began moving away from him. "See you." It was almost a quaver.

"Saturday?" was all he called, starting after her, but it was enough to make her whirl around, bump into him, and drop her books.

He kneeled beside her, piling up books, paper, notebooks.

"I thought," he said conversationally, "that we might start it nice and easy and quiet-like. Sort of get acquainted. After the game."

He got up, looking calm and solid and handed her the books which she accepted, trembling, glad of their weight because they gave her something to hold on to.

"I don't know whether it's so smart . . . you and the first game of the season all in one day," he told her.

Stephie wondered whether there was possibly, just possibly, a faint touch of excitement on his face, but she couldn't tell because he had turned her around and was half marching her out of the lunchroom and into the hall toward her class.

"But I'll chance it." He stopped her short outside Room 106. "This is it, isn't it?"

She nodded agreeably, feeling sort of happily disembodied. It could have been a manual training room for all she cared.

"Look," he added hurriedly, "I know a place, out a ways, but it's a nice drive, especially this time of year and before it gets dark, when everything's not just green. Anyway, there's this old farm house with a big fireplace and there aren't any tables or anything, just big chairs and window seats and they bring you heavy old mugs of hot chocolate . . . Okay?"

She nodded again.

He gave her a little push toward the door. "Okay," he repeated. And he left her there, walking rapidly down the hall.

Stephie stared after him until he disappeared. She took a deep breath, feeling very . . . very okay for the first time in months.

## ~§ *Chapter seventeen*

ANTICIPATION WAS A WONDERFUL THING, STEPHIE THOUGHT.
It made Wednesday's spinach taste like dessert and
Thursday's homework seem like a crossword puzzle. It
made Friday the day before SATURDAY and Friday's dress,
her new jumper, look even better on her than when she
bought it. It very nearly made her late for school, dreaming along and thinking about all the things Jim had said.

She hugged her books to her happily. Jim could make
it work. Why, she hadn't thought about Scott at all
during these past three days. Well . . . hardly at all.
And Jim was wrong about Scott's crawling back to her.
She knew it the minute she saw Scott, the dramatic dark-
ness of him, waiting at her locker with a bold impatience,
and she came up to him instead of running away.

He greeted her with a quick, characteristic gesture,
intense, demanding, always looking as if he were going
somewhere even when he was already there.

No preamble, of course. Just, "What are you doing
tonight?"

Sickened, she felt the old thumping start inside again.

"I'm . . ." Words suddenly seemed too big to fit her
throat. She wet her lips and swallowed. "I'm going to
the pep rally here at school."

He gave her his irresistible gamin look. "Same old thing . . . fight talk by the coach, seven rahs for the team, and a bonfire . . . Look, what do you say we do something else instead? I'll pick you up in front of the gym before the rally gets going."

Stephie couldn't help herself. "Yes."

And he smiled the old dizzying smile and was gone.

Crawl back? she thought dazedly. Even a trumpet fanfare wasn't for Scott. It was typical that he should just come back as though today were half a year ago yesterday.

She was still leaning weakly against the locker when Jim came by.

"I've been thinking about . . ." he began and stopped. "What's wrong?"

She turned her back quickly and began fumbling with the combination lock. "Nothing." She even managed a rueful little laugh. "I can't seem to open this darn thing today."

"Oh . . . Well, let me try it." He dropped his books on the floor. "What's the combination?"

"Eleven right," she said slowly as he whirled the dial. "Four left," thinking crazily, tell him, tell him now, so he can get out, because he'll have to. There's no room for three. It'll always be the same, this thing with Scott, so tell him. You promised.

And she told him. "Five right and two left."

Jim tugged at the lock. "That does it." He turned around. "As I was saying, I've been thinking about the pep rally tonight. Maybe I could walk you home."

She reached up and dragged a book off the shelf.

[145]

"I'm going to stay in and wash my hair." It was really quite easy when you didn't have to look at him. "Tomorrow's pretty special. Maybe we shouldn't jump the gun on it." How had she learned to dissemble? Had it always been hiding inside her? The most awful part of it all was that Jim believed her.

Stephie knew he was pleased, deep down pleased, though all he said was, "I'll pick you up at the west gate after the game. Around four thirty."

She waited until he had gone and then slammed the locker door shut defiantly.

All right, she thought, so I lied. I couldn't tell him . . . so soon . . . could I? She was wandering down the hall to her first class, but she felt as though she were running. Think about it, she told herself harshly, the least you can do is think about why you lied . . . To play it safe in case Scott didn't work out? Of course not! There was nothing to work out. Everything was the same, Barbara notwithstanding. She felt it, with Scott, with herself, and no matter how much she was attracted to Jim, Scott took precedence over everything, everybody . . . No, that wasn't the answer. Muddled, she shook her head. Well, then, think about why she gave in to Scott without a struggle, love or no love. Think about his going steady with Barbara. Think about Scott . . . and the old smile . . . that promised so much. She shivered slightly. That's all she really wanted to think about, anyway. She didn't want to think about a Stephie become a Barbara by accepting . . . about why instead of why not.

But she did, of course. Even when she was in his car that evening being driven out into the country.

[146]

He hadn't said much so far except hi and if you want the heater on say so. Nothing about Barbara. Nothing about this, tonight, Stephie and Scott together again. She expected some explanation, but the silence was as companionable as it always had been. So she made no protest when he turned on the radio and began whistling softly.

"It's a little hard to whistle to, isn't it?" She didn't really care, but it was as good as anything else she could think of to say.

"Don't you like progressive jazz? It's real cool and controlled even with all the improvisation."

"You sound like an album cover."

He thumped out a beat with his left foot.

"Listen to this . . . the base and treble sound as if they're being played in different keys."

"I guess that's why I don't like it. They never bump into each other long enough for you to catch the melody. Barbara used to say. . . ."

She stopped, horrified, trying to suck the name back in, but it didn't seem to bother him that she had mentioned it first.

"That's why I like it. You don't have time to get tired of it."

"I suppose so," she said wondering why he didn't talk about Barbara now that the name was out. "Everyone gets tired of things."

"Um . . ." was all he said, his fingers on the wheel taking up the offbeat rhythm.

And she thought, later, then, he'll talk about it later, when the setting is right.

Scott nosed the car down a hill and they came out of the trees onto a small strip of sand and the moon made faces in the water and he reached for her and his kiss was as breathtaking as it always had been and at last she relaxed in his arms . . . and still no explanation.

He touched the tip of her nose.

"You'll look the same when you're thirty . . . young and wide-eyed, right out of a fairy tale."

She laughed self-consciously. "Princesses always have long golden hair."

"But you have a golden heart."

Corny, she thought, if anybody else said it, but not Scott's saying it. With him it was right, part of his charm, the charm of a fairy tale prince. And, indeed, that's just what he had always been, though why it should disturb her now she didn't know.

She waited. But he still didn't explain anything.

And then finally, almost desperately, she said, "You mean I've got a golden heart because it's forgiving?"

He rubbed his nose in her cheek.

"Because it's good and pure. Because it's for real."

"Because it stayed faithful?" she prodded.

"It isn't a matter of staying faithful. It's always been that way, hasn't it?"

"Scott. . . ."

"Remember the time I thought you were interested in that Bill, or whatever his name was, and I told you you were my girl?"

She nodded.

"What a square I was!" he said, running his fingertips around the back of her neck. "I wouldn't have to say a goofy thing like that now, because I know you're my girl. You couldn't be anything else."

She barely shook her head because she couldn't have

done more than that, feeling his fingers evoking that special sweet kind of sleepiness you feel only when you're wide awake, knowing that even if she could have really shaken her head, she wouldn't have for fear he'd stop.

"Scott," she whispered again as he kissed the tip of her ear. "Your parents. . . ."

"What about them?" His lips moved up her cheek. "Mother's got a cold, but she'll get over it, and Dad's going to buy a new car. At least I think I've talked him into it."

"But . . . but . . ." feeling his lips all the time, all the time, moving over her forehead and down to her eyes. "But . . ." she tried once more.

"You talk too much," he murmured, as he slid his lips down on hers.

Something was wrong. She didn't feel, as she had in the past, that she had lost her identity, that she was like a kaleidoscope bursting into beautiful new shapes and colors under his lips.

She wrenched herself away, taking a deep gulp of air.

He grinned. "I guessed I haven't lost my touch if you're that breathless."

She felt a little sick. She had to say something to get him started talking about the whole miserable situation.

"How could you possibly lose your touch? You've kept in practice."

He didn't answer. Just drew her head over to him again.

She jerked up straight. "No, Scott . . . No!"

"The trouble with you," he said, "is you've been struggling with football players too long."

"I haven't been struggling with . . ." She refused to utter Jim's name. "With anyone," she said. "And you know it."

"Of course I know it. But does he? You're too considerate a person ever to tell him. You'd rather dodge and wiggle away from him than tell him that you're my girl and always will be. No matter what. You're a no-matter-what type."

"Isn't that convenient for you," she commented bitterly.

"Good for me and not good for anybody else."

"For your information," she said levelly, "he knew how I felt. He never tried to take advantage of your not being around."

"Don't give me that! He's a guy, isn't he? I know what I'd do if I had a pretty girl around, whether she was moping over some other guy or not."

She whirled on him. "Don't make him a carbon copy of yourself! Everyone isn't like you!"

"Tch, tch." He forced her back against the seat. "I can see I have to take you in hand again. You've got into some bad habits."

How, she thought wearily, allowing herself to sink against him, did we get on the subject of me? How did he maneuver it so that she was put on the defensive? But maybe it was just as well. She didn't have to have an explanation. . . .

She sighed, reluctantly deciding there was nothing much you could do about the charm of the Scotts of this world that made you give in rather than give up.

"Better, huh?" he said, lacing his fingers in hers as she relaxed on his shoulder.

"Yes."

"What do you want to do tomorrow night?"

Tomorrow! Her head stiffened on his shoulder and she squeezed her eyes shut, wishing desperately that there wasn't a Scott or a Jim and most of all a Stephie to wake up to tomorrow.

"Nothing," she finally said, opening them. "I've got a date."

"Break it."

"No."

"He's got to know sometime."

"No," she said again. "I can't. I won't."

"Look, baby . . . I know that girls don't break dates at the last minute. But this is different. You're my girl."

"No," she said for the third time. "I'm not your girl right away. Just like that. Let's go on the way we are, dating other people and dating each other and gradually work back into it."

Something in her voice made him ask half-petulantly. "Making me stand in a corner, huh?"

"No. I think we stand a better chance if we gradually work back into it."

"Okay, princess . . . It's your show. But don't keep me standing there too long."

"Meaning there are other girls who wouldn't make you wait?"

His infectious laugh drew her to him as much as his arm.

"You're too suspicious. I want you to make up your own mind, not whether it's him or me, but whether this gradually working back into things isn't a lot of bunk. However, on second thought, maybe this will help. . . ."

He kissed her again, gently, lingeringly, before putting her head back on his shoulder and starting the motor.

It should have helped, but it didn't . . . much. Why, she thought despairingly, do I do things like this? Why do I make things harder on myself? This is what I've wanted all these months, isn't it? Scott's back, so why not feel glad and gay and grateful?

Maybe he's right, she thought. Maybe I *do* want him to stand in a corner for awhile because my pride has been hurt. . . . Or maybe I *am* suspicious, and in case things do go wrong again, I'll have Jim to fall back on.

She shivered slightly, refusing to accept herself as that kind of girl. Jim would have to be told. And there'd be nothing left to fall back on, once she'd told him. It had to be the truth, she knew, remembering now, shame flooding over her, this afternoon and the lie already told.

She dug her fists into her eyes and rubbed them. There were so many things to iron out. Like Scott's telling Barbara, too. . . . Or maybe not telling Barbara. . . . It was over between them or else Scott never would have come back. Probably by mutual consent, remembering Barbara who liked boys to be cute and fun, but mostly plural.

She shivered again, wondering why this evening which had seemed so promising seemed so flat.

"Cold?" Scott asked. "I'll turn the heater on."

She merely shook her head, thinking it would surely have been better had Scott offered even a little explanation. But the closest he came to it was in front of her house when he said happily, "Just the same. Everything's just the same." And for some reason, that was the wrong explanation.

She let herself into the house quietly and stood for a moment at the half-open door watching his tail lights disappear.

"Scott," she whispered. "Scott, Scott," as though by repeating it the name would have some meaning for her.

Stephie, in her pajamas, dried her face briskly, but it still had that kiss-blurred look when she held it close to the mirror. She abruptly turned on the faucet again and splashed cold water on it. The water cleared her face somewhat but not her thoughts.

She snapped off the bathroom light and started padding back to her bedroom when she bumped into her mother in the dark hall. Stephie barely managed to stifle a shriek.

"I've been waiting for you to come out of there," her mother said anxiously. "What's the matter? Are you sick?"

"No."

"Well, what took you so long? Pep rallies don't last until one in the morning. I thought you told me Jim had to be in at ten."

Stephie slid into bed. "I wasn't with Jim, Mother."

"Oh."

But something about Stephie's face, partially averted in the pillow, and her body arched way over to one side stopped her as she half rose from the foot of the bed.

"Who were you with?"

Stephie bolted upright.

[153]

"All right, Mother, I'll say it. So it was Scott! Forbidding things doesn't solve problems."

"I didn't think there was a problem once you found out about him."

"You just don't understand," she mumbled.

Edith Rodgers grimaced. "The classic response. I don't understand because there's nothing to understand but the fact that he's vain, selfish and inconsiderate. You've outgrown him, Stephie. I thought you realized it."

Stephie looked more confused than hostile.

Her mother's face softened.

"Look, darling, I'm not playing the role of stern parent for the fun of ordering you around. I want to spare you the mistakes I made when I was your age."

"I know."

"If you know that, you're really grown up. And you should also know, then. . . ."

"Am I? Am I really grown up? I know I look it, I feel it, but for one who's so grown up, I can't do much of anything." She paused. "Except make my own decisions."

"Well, of course, darling. As I was telling you. . . ."

"Your telling me doesn't mean a thing, Mother. Your knowing that Scott is selfish and inconsiderate isn't enough. I've got to know that he never opens a car door for me, sulks when he doesn't get his own way, lied rather than tell me the truth."

Stephie didn't see the beginning of a smile on her mother's face as she continued slowly and more slowly.

"I've got to know that he takes and never gives, that

[154]

he never really thinks about anybody but himself, that he never does all the little things . . ." She stopped suddenly, and with a great effort brought her attention back to her mother. "I'm me, not you, and I've got to find out for myself. And there's nothing you can really do about it but trust me."

Edith Rodgers got up and leaned over and kissed her lightly on the cheek.

"Of course I trust you. Now go to sleep. It's late and you have a big day ahead of you tomorrow."

She snapped off the light.

Nobody knows how big, Stephie thought, as she watched the door close behind her mother. Not even Jim, yet.

## ⊷§ *Chapter eighteen*

THE TROUBLE WITH ALARM CLOCKS, STEPHIE THOUGHT groggily, is they always go off when you're asleep.

She reached over to the night table and fumbled around the back of the clock.

Ten thirty, it said. She started to slide back down under the covers. If it was ten thirty, it must be Saturday or her mother would have been in to wake her long. . .

Saturday!

Her eyes flew open. Saturday!

She jumped up, remembering, feeling it flooding through her, and ran to the window.

It was cheering weather. With just enough briskness to make you feel like rah-ing even if you were losing by a big score.

She took a quick shower and began to dress almost feverishly. She pulled the new turtle-necked sweater over her head and brushed her hair with sure, deft movements.

In spite of all the activity on the outside, she felt curiously at ease on the inside, in spite of and because of the fact that she knew she had to tell Jim about Scott and last night. Once she confessed the lie, she could confess the truth, and they could then begin being Stephie and Jim.

Her mother insisted she have something for breakfast besides half a grapefruit and toast.

"You've plenty of time," she said. "I'll make you some scrambled eggs."

Stephie wasn't surprised that she could sit calmly and eat almost as much as if it were any other Saturday. She glanced at her mother and smiled and her mother smiled back and Stephie wondered if maybe she should tell her about it going to be Jim. But she decided it wasn't really necessary because she suspected that she already knew.

Stephie wasn't surprised, either, that she could sit in the grandstand and rise and cheer lustily and, above all, keep her mind as well as her eyes on the game. That she could think and talk of only victory as she was jostled down the ramp. That she could still be calm as the crowd thinned out and she was left standing almost alone at the west gate.

She was composed even when Jim drew up to the curb and threw open the door. Until she glanced at him, fresh and scrubbed from the shower room and felt her stomach skitter. She was glad. Glad especially because of the certainty, good and whole inside her, which assured her that this was the beginning.

"Hail the conquering hero," she said shyly.

"It was too close for comfort." He might have flushed but she couldn't be sure in the four thirty light.

She knew what had to be said next. She was glad at last to be getting it out and over with. Once the bad part was admitted, the good would be so good. She felt almost gay as she opened her mouth to say it, let's duck into a side street and park for a minute, there's something I want to tell you. But before she could say it, they had already ducked and parked.

It was the first surprise she had felt all day.

"Why . . . why are we parking?"

Jim leaned back against the door and folded his arms.

"I thought maybe you might want to tell me something."

He completely unnerved her. Gone was the composure, the control, the certainty. For he knew, he knew. And how was she to make him believe that she had truly been going to tell him?

Frightened that she would handle it badly, she began to do just that.

"What are you," she blurted, "psychic?"

"I don't have to be," he said quietly. "Someone saw you getting into his car."

"I . . . I don't mean about that," she faltered, and hated herself for faltering because it had the sound of guilt. "I mean about having something to tell you. I was going to tell you but you beat me to it."

"Were you? Like you were going to wash your hair last night?"

She looked away from him. "I'm sorry." She felt the panic shrill in her voice. "But it was a shock, seeing him, hearing him say what I'd given up hope of ever hearing him say. And I was ashamed . . . ashamed of having you know I'd given in so quickly."

He sounded short of breath. "I-don't-want-to-hear-any-more." He paused for a minute and then went on more evenly. "Because if I listen, I'll believe. You have that effect." He sat up straight and wrapped his hands around the wheel with a strangling motion. "In all fairness to you, I think you should know I'm more sore at myself, because it happened too soon, before I could get my own whacks in. You were right. If I hadn't been so pig-headed about you coming to me with no strings, maybe Scott wouldn't matter now."

She dared to look at him.

"But he doesn't matter," she said urgently. "At least not in the way you think."

His hands quieted suddenly.

"What way? Either he matters or he doesn't."

She took a deep breath. "It's not that simple. That's part of what I was going to tell you. You see, it was just like when we were going together. I got in and he put his arm around me as if it were last March, and we parked close to the water, and there was a moon, a big, soft one, and. . . ."

Jim whipped around toward her.

"What are you trying to do?" he demanded. "Just tell me what the score is. I don't want details."

She backed away just a little.

"But the details are part of the score."

"Okay, okay. Say it and finish it."

"All right . . ." She plunged on. "And he kissed me. I won't say I didn't like it," she explained hurriedly, "because I did. It was . . . was almost as good as ever. But the girl was wrong."

"Wrong?"

"Nothing had changed. Everything was just the same,

as if nothing had happened, as if Barbara hadn't happened. I shouldn't say nothing, because I had changed. You just can't pick up where you left off even with an explanation."

"What did he say?"

"That's it, nothing. No explanation. And at first I thought that was what was wrong, Scott thinking he could just whistle me back and go on from there without any explanation."

"What was it, then?"

"Well, later, at home, I couldn't shake the feeling that for a wonderful evening I should be feeling more wonderful, and it suddenly dawned on me that there's more to it than kissing. You can't just love a person, you have to like him, too." She stopped and tried to swallow the dryness in her throat. "All this may not make much sense to you, but what I'm trying to say is that I like Scott all right just as I like anybody I don't hate, but not as I like you."

Jim just sat there and she became a little desperate.

"Don't you *see?*" She put her hand on his arm. "Everything was the same and it shouldn't have been. Scott is just a little boy who gets what he wants and the getting for him isn't as good as the wanting. I've outgrown him."

He took hold of her wrist. Hard.

"Maybe if you drift along with both of us, give him time, he'll change."

His grip hurt but she didn't wince.

"I don't want a sometimes dating of you and Scott," she said softly but firmly. "I want it to be all the time Jim."

[160]

"You're sure?"

"Very sure."

"One more thing." He slid his hand down gently to hers. "You and I, it won't be steady."

Her face must have shown what she felt.

"That's the first caring you've ever done about me," he told her almost fiercely. "What I mean," he finally went on, "is that it won't be the usual going steady. No tags, no commitments. If it works out, good, but we'll be free to pull out any time we want. That way we won't make as much of a mess of each other if it doesn't. I may be okay for you now but who knows what'll be okay next month, next year?"

She tried to say it lightly. "You mean I'll never know where I stand."

He moved his hands up to her shoulders.

"You'll know. Lord, yes, you'll know."

She was content with even that much. Funny, she thought, about being a senior. You didn't become one by simply passing Cicero, or being seventeen, or ordering your class ring. You had to grow into one.

*❧ Chapter nineteen*

THERE WAS MORE TO IT, STEPHIE THOUGHT, THAN BEING
in and out of love and in again. It was more than the big
thing of changing her feelings. There were all the little
things like changing the pictures in her wallet, the one of
Scott standing tall on the steps of the library because
she had taken it at the bottom and the one of them both
on the beach, a good one of Scott, thin, intense, quick-
smiled, the little-boy devil look about him. It meant
changing to higher heels, wearing softer colors, adapting
to another style of dancing. It meant learning to talk
about different things, learning to sense different nuances
in speech and gestures, learning new concepts of what
was what. But it was worth it.

It was kind of sad, though, this doing off with the old
so you could get on with the new. She picked up a pile
of old letters, started to open the top one, hesitated, and
instead tore it once across. Finished. The rest of the pile
followed.

Done. She made herself get up and rummage through
her dresser drawer. She dropped the charm bracelet Scott
had given her one Christmas into a box, rummaged again
and found his B.A.A. club pin and a stuffed dog he had

won for her at a carnival, and put these in also. She sighed and snapped a rubber band around the box. File away and forget.

She moved back to her desk and sat down rather limply. Over, she thought. . . . But where do you file and forget your first kiss, first date, first dance?

She was still sitting there, looking and feeling vacant when her mother poked her head in the doorway.

"Stephie, are you in . . . Oh, there you are. What are you doing?"

Stephie looked up vaguely. "I was cleaning out my desk." She turned around and picked up the snapshot of herself and Scott. "Look . . . Did I really look like this?"

Her mother peered over her shoulder. "Oh, you weren't that bad. A little bony and freckled, maybe." She straightened, resting her hand for a moment on Stephie's shoulder. "You're not still mooning over him?" she asked uneasily.

Yes, Stephie thought, and no. But she couldn't very well say that to her mother without explaining, and some things you couldn't explain out loud. How explain that you could moon over the once had been *being* once had been and still be glad that the might have been wasn't? Moon over some things, the look of him, the quick sweet smile, the little-boy eyes that always looked as though they were getting into something. Not moon over other things, the possessiveness, the petulance, the pretense that he wanted her when he wanted Barbara. Certainly not moon over the shame of wanting him until, strangely enough, he, himself, destroyed the want by fulfilling it.

"Well?" her mother asked.

[163]

Stephie started. "Well, what?"

"You're not still mooning over him?" she repeated.

Stephie shook her head because the time for mooning was past. The time now was for telling, telling Scott that Stephie and Scott were no longer Stephie and Scott. He should have been told before this, but somehow the moment was never right. And it had to be right. And somehow it had to be softened so there'd be no bitterness to ruin the memories. For both of them.

"I . . . I like Jim, Stephie," her mother said softly and a little timidly, bringing her back to now, this moment of now. Stephie smiled up at her. Once a mother's recommendation would have been anathema. But not now.

"Guess what?" she said, "I do, too."

Stephie checked everything the next morning before she left for school. Theme for Advanced Comp . . . History text . . . pen . . . wallet. She took time to glance at the picture of Jim she had inserted in it last night and then quickly stuffed the wallet back in her purse.

She'd have to talk to him about that, she thought, as she hurried down two blocks, over three, and up one. What other girl had to carry a picture torn from the sports section of the school paper? And one, at that, which could have been six other people for all it showed of his face. The bigness was there, all right, but no sandy brush of hair, no strong gray eyes, no little line squiggling down one corner of his mouth betraying the purposeful once-in-awhile smile.

She reached her locker a full two minutes early. She tossed in her history text thinking, he wasn't the kind,

[164]

even if she had a personal snapshot of him, to make it really personal. He'd never write even Love, Jim. Maybe Jim, he would, but that was all. She didn't really care, because as he told her she'd know where she stood, and she did, he wasn't shy about it at all when they were alone. It was just that it would be kind of nice to be able to open her wallet and read even a Love, Jim, and know she wasn't dreaming.

Of course, the school paper helped. She was reading it in the drugstore after her last class while waiting for Jim. A sentence in The Tattler about what star back doesn't mind being on the bench as long as it's in the park next to Stephie. She blushed, happily embarrassed.

"Reading your press notices?"

She blushed again. "Hi, Scott." She hastily folded the paper and slipped it under her books.

He slid into the booth opposite her. "You're not going to get out of it that easy." He gestured toward the paper. "You can't run away from yourself forever."

She was startled. "Myself?"

"Look . . ." He leaned toward her intimately. "You don't have to put on an act with me. I'm Scott, remember? So, don't pretend. I know how you feel. How you've always felt."

Outraged, Stephie clenched her hands to keep them from trembling. "So, you know how I feel, how I've always felt," she said, the anger beating out each word hard and strong. "Tell me, how did I feel last May when we broke up, last August when I found you out, and last month when you decided to fall like a little autumn leaf back into my life again?"

[165]

He grinned. "I fall hard, not lightly. I fell hard for you."

"And my Best Friend and any other girl that might come along."

"Okay, so I was wrong," he said in his most persuasive little boy soft sorry voice. "How long are you going to make me stand in the corner?"

"Jim and I . . ." she began.

"You're not going steady, are you?"

"No . . ." Which was true, of course, but she found she couldn't, after all, go into the long explanation until the moment was right. And, somehow, she wondered if there was a moment, now or ever, when it would be right.

"No," she said again, "but. . . ."

He cut her off. "Here comes our star back now." He got up and leaned over her. "I'll go along with the punishment," he said quickly, "if it's necessary to save your girlish pride or something, but remember," he added softly, "don't keep me waiting too long."

He straightened, nodded at Jim, and sauntered away.

Jim dropped down into the booth.

"What was that all about?"

"Tired?"

"Sort of."

"Oh."

"Oh, what?"

She gestured vaguely at the crowded booths and tried to talk over the noise.

"Oh, I thought that if the coach didn't run you ragged

this afternoon, we could get out of this and take a walk. Like home. The long way, through the park."

His smile was slow, as it always was, warming as it crept over his face and up to his eyes.

"You must believe everything you read, like my fondness for park benches."

She felt herself blushing again.

"Well, whether you want to be tagged or not, we are. Everyone believes The Tattler," she said lightly.

"Not Scott, obviously, from the look he gave me just now." He stretched, looking a little amused. "And tired as I am I want you to know I'm not so tired that I didn't know you changed the subject before."

She smiled. "I know." And then the smile dropped away. "If I wasn't so mad I'd laugh about it."

He got up and pulled her to her feet.

"C'mon, then. Let's walk off the mad and laugh about it together."

But they didn't laugh about it, of course.

"He thinks I'm punishing him," she sputtered helplessly as they scuffed through the leaves in the park. "That you're just a temporary tit for tat thing while I'm soothing my ego." She put her hand on his arm apologetically. "And it's not just you. It could be anybody. He really doesn't give you a second thought."

"You didn't tell him." It was as close to an accusation as he'd ever get.

"Tell him what? That we're going steady when we're not? He'd never understand it."

"No." He took her hand. "You should tell him that

[167]

maybe we're growing into something, you and I. Going steady . . . that's kid stuff."

They turned into the path winding toward an old wooden bridge which humped across a lagoon.

"I was going to tell him that," futility in her voice, her eyes, "but I knew he wouldn't believe me. He isn't ready to believe it yet."

Jim picked up a stone and threw it hard into the water.

"Do you want me to tell him to lay off?"

She shook her head. "Thanks. No, it's up to me. And besides, he'd never, never believe you. You'd only convince him that I was trying to make him jealous."

She leaned her elbows on the bridge railing and stared down at her contorted reflection.

"Funny, isn't it," she said, "how things change. I've gone a complete circle with Scott from caring to not caring. Once I would have died if I ever thought things would change.

Jim dropped an arm around her waist and leaned over the railing with her.

"You know," she told him with a sigh of content, "it's different with you. It's not like when I was going steady with Scott and was so bored I didn't know what to do, though I was afraid to admit it. I thought the boredom was just part of growing up."

He rumpled her hair.

"Give me time. I may bore you as you've never been bored before."

"No." She was emphatic. "With you, there's always something to talk about. And . . . and kissing's secondary."

He jerked upright. "I can see I've got to correct that

impression right away." He pushed her head down and held it there, running his lips over the back of her neck.

She giggled. "Stop it, that tickles!" And giggled again. "Stop it, Jim, I'm serious!"

"Not until you say uncle, or better yet, Jim, in an appreciative throbbing tone of voice."

"All right!" she squeeled. "Jim, Jim!"

"Not good enough."

"Well, it's hard to throb upside down over a railing!"

"Okay." He released her. "I'm waiting."

"Jim," she said breathlessly, and not just from having been put right side up. "You know what I meant, anyway."

He led her over to a bench and she curled up beside him.

"I'm beginning to believe my publicity," he said. "The Tattler's got something."

She stirred against him.

"You know, I'm glad Scott came back. It was the only way I'd ever have really known he didn't matter."

"But he matters now," he said somewhat impatiently. "To me, anyway. Hanging around, making a pest of himself."

There was a trace of laughter on her breath. "Jealous?"

"No. With you and me, jealousy's no good." He kicked restlessly at a pile of leaves at his feet. "Maybe if he's laughed at long enough he'll stop," he added finally. "But I doubt it."

There was no fun in her eyes now. "Laughed at?" she repeated.

"Sure. Everyone knows about you and me and if he's

[169]

so much in love with himself that he refuses to see it, well, he has to expect to be laughed at." He got up, leaned down and raised her to her feet, his hands hard on her shoulders. "Do you mind?"

"Yes," she admitted simply. "I can't hate him, Jim, and I don't think you'd want me to. Scott will always be a little special, like Santa Claus. You outgrow it but you can't throw away the memory of the first time you were sure you heard something on the roof." She dropped her eyes. "Laughter can be terrible, especially for someone like Scott. I know it sounds funny, but I don't want him laughed at."

He kissed the tip of her nose.

"No wonder I wanted you for my girl. Don't worry. I don't think anything will ever break him, not laughter, anyway. But I'm not like you. I don't care what it takes to make him go away. I just wish he'd go, that's all."

She wrapped her arms around his waist and dug her head in his chest.

"He will, Jim. How could he possibly not be aware of us? Everyone else is."

# ❧ Chapter twenty

STEPHIE WAS RIGHT. EVERYONE ELSE CERTAINLY WAS aware of the way things were with herself and Jim. Always together. Never farther apart than a hyphen in the school gossip column which always referred to them as the Rodgers-Stuart combine.

Even Barbara, of course. No, not of course, at all, Stephie thought. Supposed would be more like it, because she didn't know anything of course about Barbara at all any more. Once she would have known when Barbara got a new dress, or what Barbara said to Mac when she broke a date with him, or why Barbara decided to elect Typing rather than Twentieth Century Poetry.

Those things Stephie knew, once knew, except what made her tick inside . . . The inside ticking . . . Stephie smiled at the follow-up thought, though it really wasn't funny at all. The inside ticking . . . Like a mattress. Barbara, she thought, should really wear one of those tags . . . This person consists of 31% charm, 23% selfishness, 19% hypocrisy. This tag is attached as a certification that this person is as represented . . . That would do it.

Stephie stooped and put her books on the sidewalk in

order to button the hood of her jacket at the throat. She picked them up and again bent against the pushing cold of the late November afternoon.

It would do it, all right, she thought, but it wouldn't do. At all. Because it was unfair, really, to tag anybody or anything except a mattress or a blouse with washing instructions. No tag could truly represent anybody. Even Barbara.

Stephie shivered a little and guessed it was just as well that she didn't know anything of course about Barbara any more. She passed Bronson's and was half a block beyond it when Barbara puffed up beside her.

"I thought it was you," she said breathlessly. "Golly, it's cold, isn't it?"

"Yes," Stephie agreed indifferently.

Barbara bounced along next to her.

"Well, you sure don't seem surprised to see me."

"I see you."

Barbara looked flustered, if Stephie had bothered to look.

"I mean, we don't see much of each other any more."

"No."

Silence, and the bounce perceptively lessened. Then, "Want to go back for a Coke?" Barbara put into the silence.

"I don't think so."

"Well how about a . . . a hot chocolate?" she said brightly, which should have been underscored by a snap of the fingers if she didn't have mittens on. "It'll warm us up."

"No."

"I see." Anger in the seeing. "You don't want a Coke, you don't want a hot chocolate . . . with me! You don't want anything with me!"

Stephie thought of holding back, it was harder to hurt than not to, not hurting was the easy way out, and decided against it.

"No, I guess I don't," she said levelly.

"Then you are mad! I supposed you were, but there're two sides to everything, you know!"

"I'm not mad," Stephie said quietly, reminded suddenly with sad amusement of the old time when she had been so very, very, very careful not to get Barbara mad, and all the times when she had, and had cajoled, pleaded, placated that anger.

Barbara looked at her curiously.

"I don't think you really are." She tried to loop her arm through Stephie's, but Stephie's books interfered. "We had lots of good times together, Stephie. We can still. . . ."

Stephie cut in sharply.

"No, we can't."

Barbara's voice was that of a thwarted child.

"You must be mad. And I don't blame you. But I didn't do it on purpose. Things just . . . just happened. I wouldn't do a thing like that on purpose. You're my Best Friend. At first, I didn't even like him, then. . . ."

Stephie shook her head and kept on shaking it.

"I don't want to hear it," she said in a monotone, almost afraid she'd weaken, the habit was still so strong, if Barbara heard anything to take advantage of in the tone of her voice. "Don't tell me."

[173]

But Barbara did. She went on as though she had never been interrupted.

"And then I began to like him all right, the four of us had a lot of fun together, or the three of us, Mac didn't really count. And then, suddenly, when he'd pull me up from a chair, or something like that, he was pulling but it wasn't pulling, it was holding my hand, and I was you not me. I wasn't as I always was, just with a boy and looking for something, anything to make whatever we were doing seem better than it was. I was you because he treated me like you. So you just can't be mad, not now, not any more."

Stephie stopped and faced her, the wind whipping leaves, skirts, hats, everything but her words into a frenzy.

"Can't you understand?" she asked wearily. "I'm not mad. I'm not anything. I don't even feel sorry for you. I just don't feel anything."

Shock and realization that Stephie really didn't lumped together on Barbara's face and then blended into indifference.

"Mind if I walk along with you, anyway?" she asked.

Now what? Stephie thought, walking on rapidly. Barbara didn't believe anyone could ever feel nothing for her, least of all Stephie, but now that she knew, she really didn't care, Stephie saw. All the good years of feeling things together didn't make any difference to her. Barbara could have been the Best Friend of anybody who lived next door.

"You certainly are lucky to have Jim," Barbara said. "He's. . . ."

And Stephie, remembering Barbara's estimation once of how lucky she was to have Scott, spun on her.

"Leave Jim out of it! I'm warning you, Barbara. If you ever go after Jim the way you did Scott, I'll fight. This time I'll fight!"

Barbara had the grace to flush.

"I don't want Jim. I want Scott."

And then it came out. The reason for the attempt to make up.

"You have Jim," she flung at her. "What do you want Scott hanging around for, too?"

Stephie stared at her, truly perplexed, and then it struck her.

"Oh, no," she breathed, "no!" And she began to laugh, filling up with it, spilling over with it, making the people passing by smile tolerantly, wistfully.

"Stop it!" Barbara hissed. "Everyone's looking at us! What's so funny, anyway?"

"I'm sorry," she gasped. "I just never thought I'd see you ground down to size."

"So I like him! What's so funny about that?"

Stephie gulped down a fresh wave of laughter. "Nothing," she said, only a smile left of the laughter. "I'm laughing at myself, really. Laughing at all the time I spent crying over him. You two didn't really break up, did you?"

"You know that as well as I do! You just look at him cross-eyed and he comes running!"

"I haven't looked at him any way in a long time."

"Maybe not now, now that you've got Jim. But you

did, you must have, you must have said something or else he wouldn't have dropped me without a word!"

"Maybe no word's better than a lie."

Barbara heard that but you wouldn't have known she did.

"Look, Stephie," she said ingratiatingly, "you always were the nicest person I ever knew. I know you don't care any old way about me any more, but you could, just because you're nice, you could tell him. Tell him you like Jim. One word from you. . . ."

"And he'll do as he pleases," Stephie cut in, embarrassed for her. She gently put her hand on her arm. "He'll never believe me. But I wish you would. Truly I do."

But Barbara couldn't and wouldn't.

"You could send him back if you wanted to! But you won't. This is your way of getting back at me because he always wanted me in the first place! Every time he dated you he was planning how he could get away early to see me! Me! You don't want him but you'll keep him around just to. . . ."

"You can have him!"

Stephie almost ran away from the hate and craziness in Barbara's voice and up the steps of her own house.

But she turned around at the top and yelled over the still outpouring venom.

"On second thought, you can't have him. Don't you know that by now? Nobody can have him. Only Scott can have Scott."


"Carefree youth." Edith Rodgers said, glancing out the window at the darkening sky. "Do you ever wish

[176]

you were seventeen again when everything and everybody is simply wonderful?"

"Nope. I don't even wish I were forty again." Tom Rodgers took the bottom shelf out of the refrigerator and shoved the turkey in. "You've certainly changed your tune. As I recall, a couple of months ago and for some time before that you thought it was a horrible age."

"I still do." She turned away from the window and began crumbling bread into a large pan already half-filled. "But kids are so resilient. They snap right back. They care a lot and then don't care."

He walked over to her and kissed the nape of her neck.

She smiled up at him. "We do have a lot to be thankful for, don't we? Stephie's had a few problems, but that's the beauty of being seventeen. What's a problem one time isn't the next."

He dropped an arm around her. "Jim's working out well, isn't he?"

"Yes. She has everything she wants . . . for the moment, anyway."

He straightened up and dragged a chair over to her.

"Kids have so much today," he said, sitting down and drawing the pan of bread crumbs between them. "And get it with so little effort."

"Break it up smaller, Tom. Crumble it like this."

"When I was young," he said, still crumbling it like that instead of this, "I was made to shoulder the responsibility of my privileges. My father was really a very wise old gent."

She smiled. "Funny how much wisdom your father

[177]

picked up between your seventeenth birthday and your forty-first."

He grinned. "Okay, I surrender! No more gripes about the younger generation."

"Your gripe isn't with the younger generation. It's with the older generation . . . us. So if the younger generation is coming to anything, it's to what the older generation has already come to."

"Our heirs inheriting our handiwork, hmm?"

But she was at the window again.

"That's what I mean," she said over the slam of the front door. "There goes Barbara cutting through the lot next door. She must have walked home with Stephie. They've made up. Everybody's nice again. And your father notwithstanding, I don't think you'd want Stephie to be any other way."

He dried his hands and threw down the towel.

"How could she think Barbara's nice again?"

"Carefree youth," Edith Rodgers said.

# ❧ Chapter twenty-one

STEPHIE WASN'T MISTAKEN ABOUT SCOTT, EITHER. HE obviously was very much aware of herself and Jim. He tried sulking. He tried making her jealous. He was in between tries the afternoon of the mixer in the gym.

When the waltz contest was announced Stephie was watching the clock and the door for Jim, who was delayed because of a make-up exam.

She wasn't surprised when Scott walked up, put his arms around her and danced her off the edge of the floor into the middle without saying a word. There was no time, really, for surprise or protest, either, and rather than embarrass them both she merely half-shrugged when he whispered, "Don't put your face close to mine. Keep your hand on my shoulder. Hold your body erect and at least six inches away from mine. No fancy steps. And smile. Keep smiling."

She smiled. There was no tenseness in it, no nervousness in her movements for she knew they'd win. Because Scott wanted to. And while the miniature trophies were being presented to them, the thought occurred to her again that the only one to whom anyone could ever lose Scott was himself.

Stephie didn't wait any longer for Jim. He'd said that if he didn't make it for the mixer, he'd pick her up at eight thirty for a movie. She slipped quietly away from the congratulatory crowd and went home.

When the doorbell rang, Stephie answered it herself.

"Hi," Scott said.

"Oh . . . Come in."

"Get your coat and we'll go some place where we can talk."

"We can talk here."

Scott smiled disarmingly and put out his hand.

"C'mon, Stephie. Haven't I been on probation long enough?"

She backed away from him.

"What do we have to talk about that can't be said here?"

His smile vanished as he followed her inside, glancing furtively around. "You know as well as I do. Us. Why did you run away today after we won? Nothing is good when we're not together."

She turned her back to him and looked out the window, not seeing anything. So, it had come, after all, the time for telling.

"Nothing's been good with us for a long time."

Scott walked quickly over to her and put his hands on her shoulders.

"It was once. Look . . ." She turned slowly under the pressure of his hands. "Do you remember how it started? That Sunday in January when you wore a red dress and. . . ."

". . . my heart on my sleeve," she finished matter-of-factly.

[180]

"See? You can't get away from it." He traced a finger over her lips. "Remember our first date?"

"Yes. . . ."

"You *do* remember, don't you," he went on just a little uncertainly, "the dances and picnics and movies and . . . everything?"

"Yes," she said wonderingly. "It was good once, wasn't it?"

"It can be again. . . ."

"No . . ." She slid out of his arms and walked to the other end of the room. "No, it can't."

He whirled around. "There isn't anyone else. Certainly not Jim! You're using him to teach me a lesson."

She took a deep breath. "Certainly Jim. Jim today, maybe Jim tomorrow."

He came toward her angrily. "If you're playing games . . . If this is your idea of revenge. . . ."

She stood there quietly and waited for him.

"I can't tell you for sure. Right now it's Jim. Maybe tomorrow and all the rest of them it'll be Jim. I hope so. Though maybe it's a Jim I haven't met yet."

"But not Scott, never Scott, is that it?"

She put her hand on his arm. "Look," she entreated, "you, too, remember how it began and how it grew into something wonderful and. . . ."

". . . this is how it ends?"

"No. There is no ending. You were the first for me and I was the first for you."

He jerked his arm away from her.

"Don't give me double-talk! Is this a brush-off . . . yes or no?"

[181]

"No brush-off, Scott," she said quietly. "All the things that made us . . . well, *us*, you and me . . . can't be brushed off. You'll see."

"All I see," he said sullenly, "is that you've decided no pay-off, no coming back. What do you want me to do, get down on my knees and beg? Will that satisfy you?"

She put out her hands as though she could stop what he'd never do anyway.

"Well, then," he demanded, "maybe you want me to say something like I'm sorry."

"Are you?"

"Yes!"

"I . . . I meant . . . meant are you saying it?"

"I just said it, didn't I? How many times do you want me to say it, five hundred times like when I was bad in grammar school? I'm sorry, I'm sorry, I'm. . . ."

"Don't, Scott. . . ."

"Isn't that what you really want, to hear me say I'm sorry about Barbara, sorry I lied to you, eat humble pie?"

"No," she said softly. "No. I can't make you pay for the rest of your life for lying. I've lied, too. Everyone lies. No, it's not the lying."

"No," he mimicked sweetly, "no . . . Can't you do anything but act wounded? Why don't you get mad and stamp your feet and holler?"

Her hands made a helpless gesture.

"I can't get mad, Scott. You can only get mad at someone you care about."

His face went white, hearing the truth in her voice.

"You'll be sorry!" He spit it out, Stephie half expecting him to stick out his tongue and add, "Yanh!"

He yanked open the door and flung back again, "You'll be sorry!" waiting for the giving in which didn't come before he slammed it.

"That woman can talk longer than any female I know!" Stephie's mother exclaimed. "Sometimes I just dread answering the phone . . . Who was that, by the way?"

"Scott."

Stephie walked into bedroom and began combing her hair.

Her mother followed her.

"I hope . . ." she began and began again, "I hope . . . that's not starting all over again."

"That," Stephie said, putting on fresh lipstick, "can only start once."

"Don't be flippant, Stephie!" Then, anxiously, "It's over, isn't it?"

Stephie smiled at her mother in the mirror. "Finished. Not over." She turned around and kissed her lightly on the cheek. "There's a difference."

And that's how it didn't end . . . Always to be remembered, nothing ever to be remembered quite like that. No matter how many times the same things are done. Never the same. Never the same as the first time, the young time, the tender time. The only time such memory-making can be significant . . . That's how it didn't end. With Stephie and Scott.

*About the Author*:

Denise Cass Brookman was born in Chicago and has lived

most of her life in that area. In 1941 she married an aviator and after the war she and her husband returned to Northwestern University where she was president of the Manuscript Club and contributed to the university's two literary magazines. The daughter of a professional writer, Mrs. Brookman began writing poetry at the age of nine and has kept at it. Her serious writing career began in 1951 when she sold her first short story to *Seventeen*.

She and her husband, now an advertising account executive, live in Barrington, Illinois, about fifty miles from Chicago, surrounded by their two children, Geoffrey and Samantha, Brutus, an English bulldog, Henry, a parakeet, and a wildlife sanctuary for rabbits, chipmunks, owls and an occasional raccoon. Besides managing this lively menagerie, Mrs. Brookman is fond of painting and designing home accessories.